6/17

AVENGERS K #4
AVENGERS VS. ULTRON

The Avengers believed Ultron, their greatest enemy, had been destroyed. But he had secretly programmed his rebellious creation the Vision, who had joined the Avengers, to retrieve the pieces of his armored body and rebuild him. Ultron attacked the Avengers and has set in motion a plan to destroy the Earth. It's up to the Vision to stop him— but can his fellow Avengers still trust him?

JIM ZUB
SCRIPT

WOO BIN CHOI with **JAE SUNG LEE, MIN JU LEE, JAE WOONG LEE, HEE YE CHO, JI HEE CHOI,** and **IN YOUNG LEE**
ART

VC's CORY PETIT
LETTERS

WOO BIN CHOI with
JAE SUNG LEE and **MYOUNG HUI LEE**
COVER ART

WOO CHUL LEE
VARIANT COVER ART

AVENGERS VS. ULTRON is adapted from AGE OF ULTRON #10AI; AVENGERS ORIGINS: VISION (2012) #1; and AVENGERS (1963) #57, #67, and #161-162.
Adaptations written by SI YEON PARK and translated by JI EUN PARK

AVENGERS created by STAN LEE and JACK KIRBY

Original comics written by MARK WAID, KYLE HIGGINS, ALEC SIEGEL, ROY THOMAS, and JIM SHOOTER; and illustrated by ANDRÉ LIMA ARAÚJO, STÉPHANE PERGER, JOHN BUSCEMA, BARRY WINDSOR-SMITH, and GEORGE PÉREZ

Editor SARAH BRUNSTAD
Manager, Licensed Publishing JEFF REINGOLD
VP, Brand Management & Development, Asia C.B. CEBULSKI
VP, Production & Special Projects JEFF YOUNGQUIST
SVP Print, Sales & Marketing DAVID GABRIEL
Associate Manager, Digital Assets JOE HOCHSTEIN
Associate Managing Editor ALEX STARBUCK
Editors, Special Projects JENNIFER GRÜNWALD   MARK D. BEAZLEY
Book Designer ADAM DEL RE

Editor in Chief AXEL ALONSO
Chief Creative Officer JOE QUESADA
Publisher DAN BUCKLEY
Executive Producer ALAN FINE

MARVEL

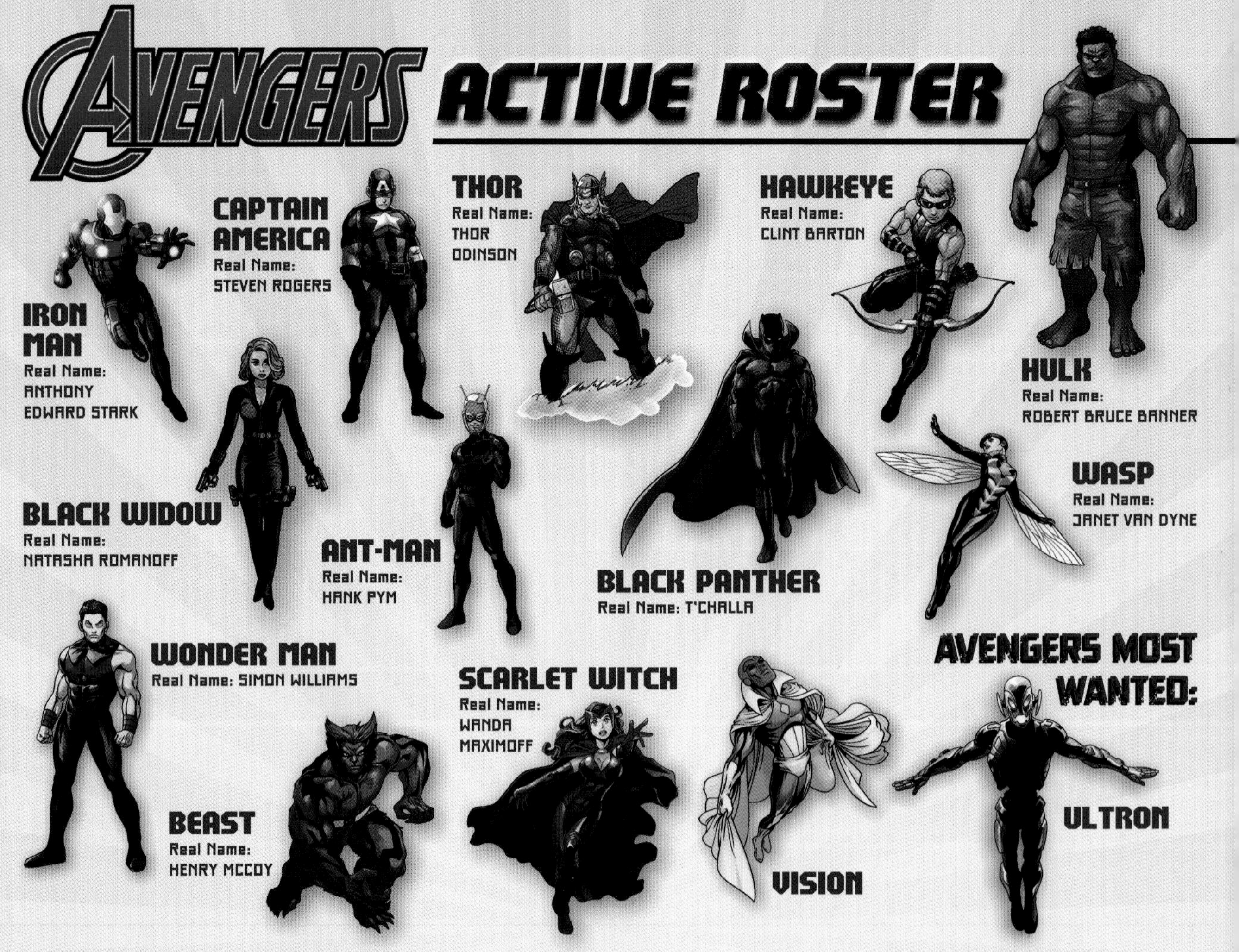
AVENGERS
ACTIVE ROSTER
IRON MAN
Real Name:
ANTHONY EDWARD STARK
CAPTAIN AMERICA
Real Name:
STEVEN ROGERS
THOR
Real Name:
THOR ODINSON
HAWKEYE
Real Name:
CLINT BARTON
HULK
Real Name:
ROBERT BRUCE BANNER
BLACK WIDOW
Real Name:
NATASHA ROMANOFF
ANT-MAN
Real Name:
HANK PYM
BLACK PANTHER
Real Name: T'CHALLA
WASP
Real Name:
JANET VAN DYNE
WONDER MAN
Real Name: SIMON WILLIAMS
SCARLET WITCH
Real Name:
WANDA MAXIMOFF
BEAST
Real Name:
HENRY MCCOY
VISION
AVENGERS MOST WANTED:
ULTRON

ABDOPUBLISHING.COM

Reinforced library bound edition published in 2017 by Spotlight, a division of ABDO, PO Box 398166, Minneapolis, Minnesota 55439.
Spotlight produces high-quality reinforced library bound editions for schools and libraries. Published by agreement with Marvel Characters, Inc.
Printed in the United States of America, North Mankato, Minnesota.
092016 012017

MARVEL
marvelkids.com

THIS BOOK CONTAINS RECYCLED MATERIALS

PUBLISHER'S CATALOGING IN PUBLICATION DATA

Names: Zub, Jim, author. | Choi, Woo Bin ; Lee, Jae Sung ; Lee, Min Ju; Lee, Jae Woong ; Cho, Hee Ye ; Choi, Ji Hee ; Lee, In Young, illustrators.
Title: Avengers vs. Ultron / writer: Jim Zub ; art: Woo Bin Choi ; Jae Sung Lee ; Min Ju Lee ; Jae Woong Lee, Hee Ye Cho, Ji Hee Choi, In Young Lee.
Description: Reinforced library bound edition. | Minneapolis, Minnesota : Spotlight, 2017. | Series: Avengers K
Summary: Ant-Man, Iron Man, Captain America, Thor, Hawkeye, and other fan-favorite Avengers take on Ultron as he plots to destroy the world.
Identifiers: LCCN 2016941682 | ISBN 9781614795681 (v.1 ; lib. bdg.) | ISBN 9781614795698 (v.2 ; lib. bdg.) | ISBN 9781614795704 (v.3 ; lib. bdg.) | ISBN 9781614795711 (v.4 ; lib. bdg.) | ISBN 9781614795728 (v.5 ; lib. bdg.) | ISBN 9781614795735 (v.6 ; lib. bdg.)
Subjects: LCSH: Avengers (Fictitious characters)--Juvenile fiction. | Super heroes--Juvenile fiction. | Comic books, strips, etc.--Juvenile fiction. | Graphic novels--Juvenile fiction.
Classification: DDC 741.5--dc23
LC record available at https://lccn.loc.gov/2016941682

ABDO
Spotlight
A Division of ABDO
abdopublishing.com

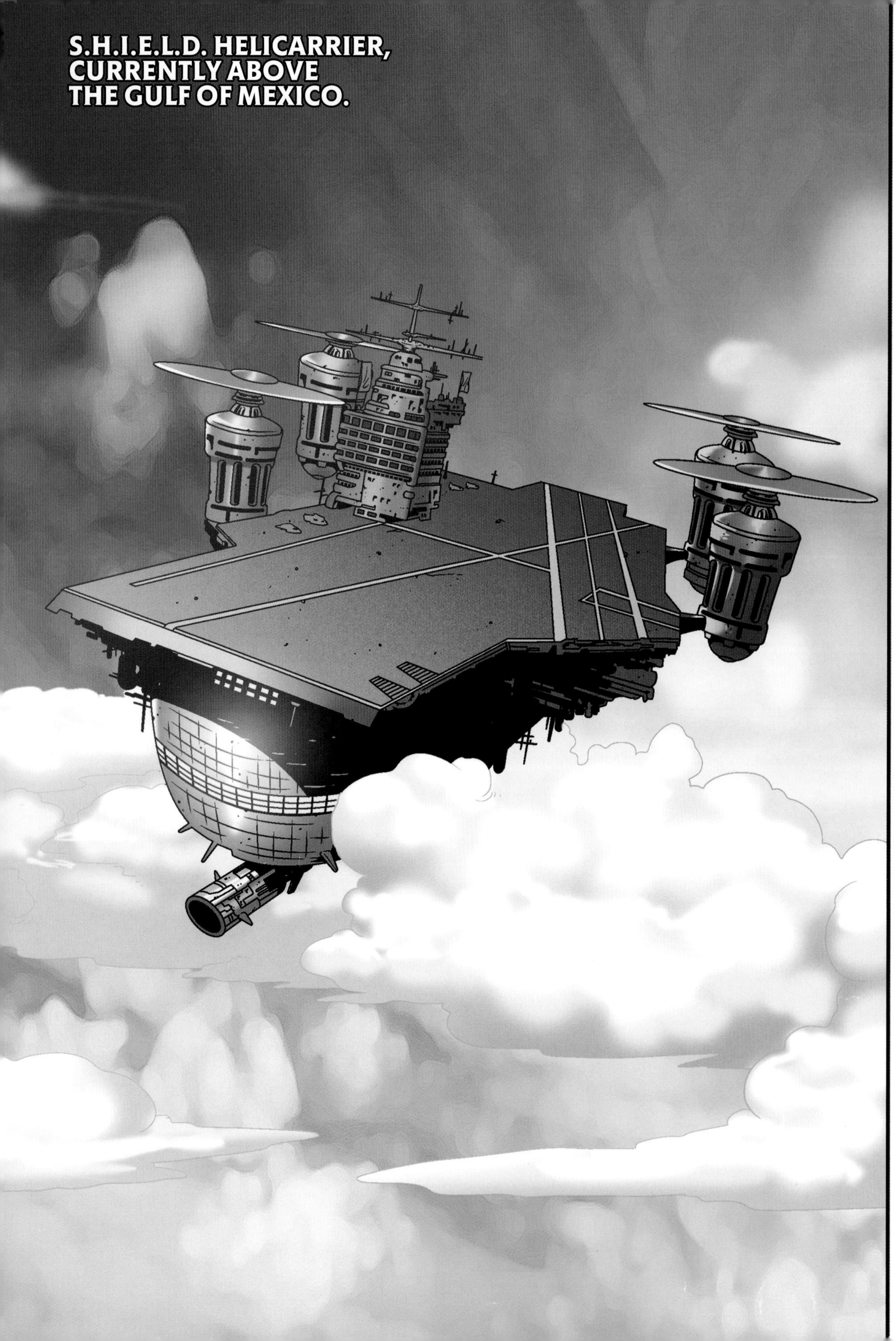
S.H.I.E.L.D. HELICARRIER, CURRENTLY ABOVE THE GULF OF MEXICO.

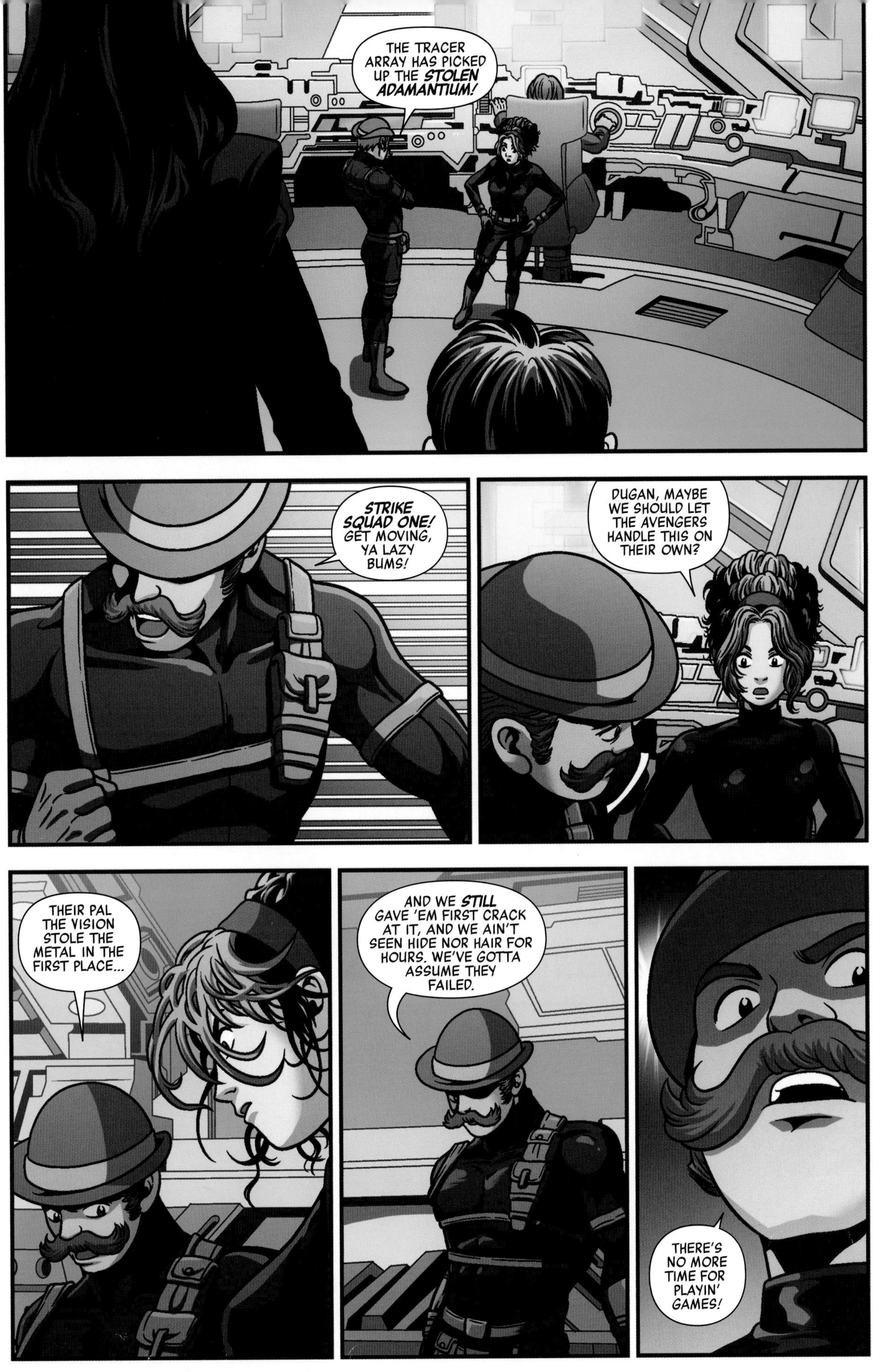
THE TRACER ARRAY HAS PICKED UP THE STOLEN ADAMANTIUM!
STRIKE SQUAD ONE! GET MOVING, YA LAZY BUMS!
DUGAN, MAYBE WE SHOULD LET THE AVENGERS HANDLE THIS ON THEIR OWN?
THEIR PAL THE VISION STOLE THE METAL IN THE FIRST PLACE...
AND WE STILL GAVE 'EM FIRST CRACK AT IT, AND WE AIN'T SEEN HIDE NOR HAIR FOR HOURS. WE'VE GOTTA ASSUME THEY FAILED.
THERE'S NO MORE TIME FOR PLAYIN' GAMES!

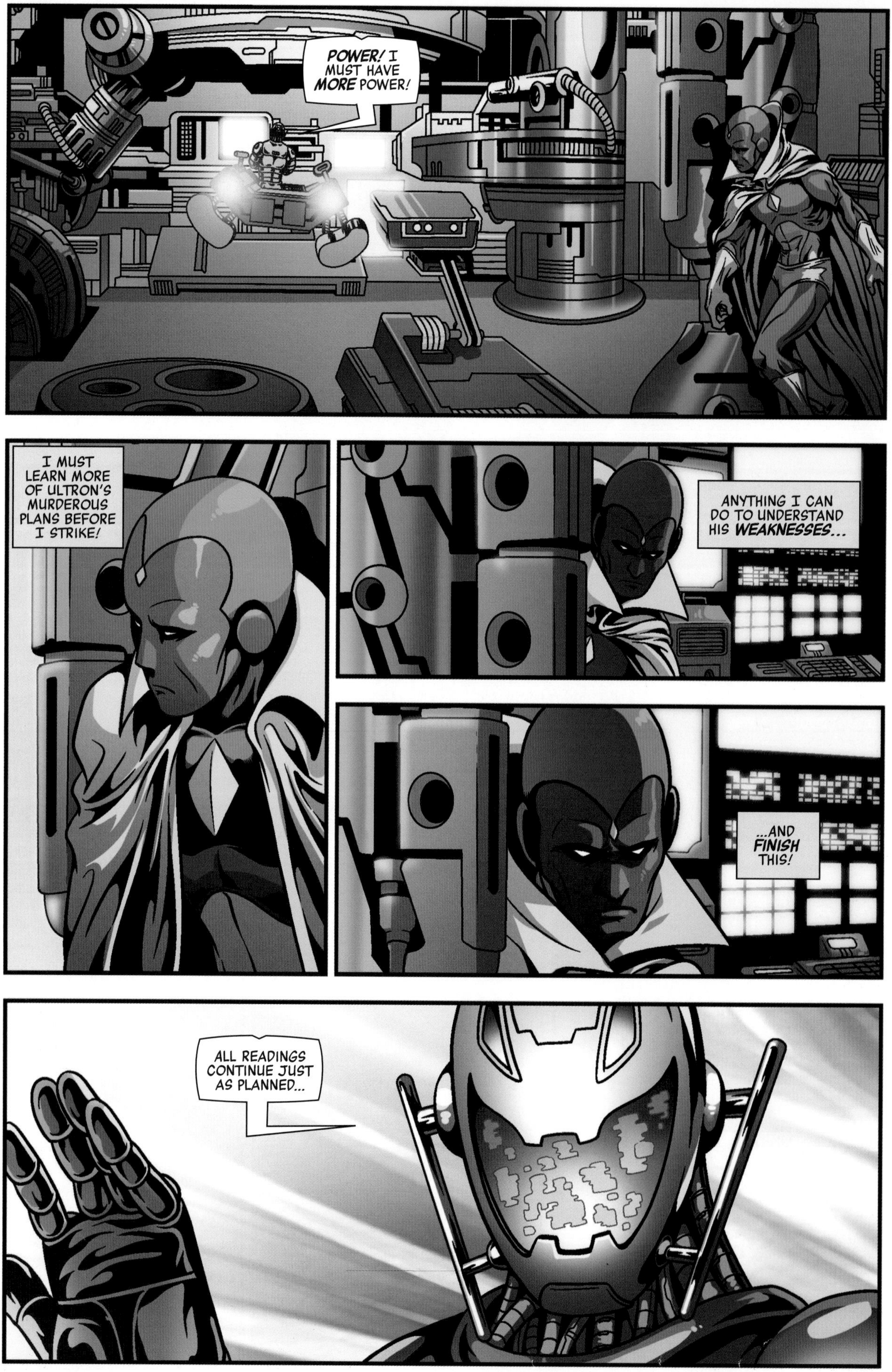
POWER! I MUST HAVE MORE POWER!
I MUST LEARN MORE OF ULTRON'S MURDEROUS PLANS BEFORE I STRIKE!
ANYTHING I CAN DO TO UNDERSTAND HIS WEAKNESSES...
...AND FINISH THIS!
ALL READINGS CONTINUE JUST AS PLANNED...

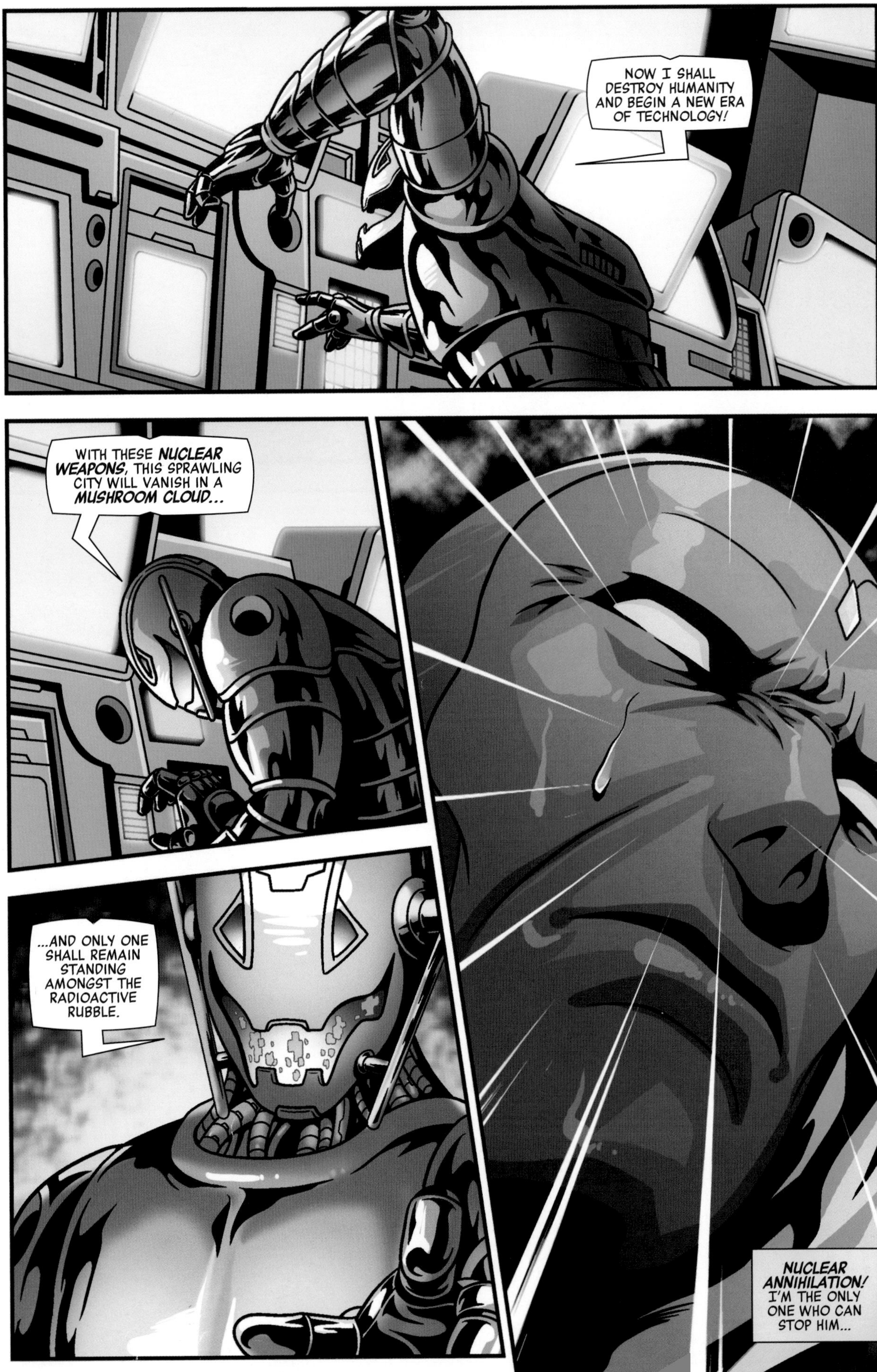
NOW I SHALL DESTROY HUMANITY AND BEGIN A NEW ERA OF TECHNOLOGY!
WITH THESE NUCLEAR WEAPONS, THIS SPRAWLING CITY WILL VANISH IN A MUSHROOM CLOUD...
...AND ONLY ONE SHALL REMAIN STANDING AMONGST THE RADIOACTIVE RUBBLE.
NUCLEAR ANNIHILATION! I'M THE ONLY ONE WHO CAN STOP HIM...

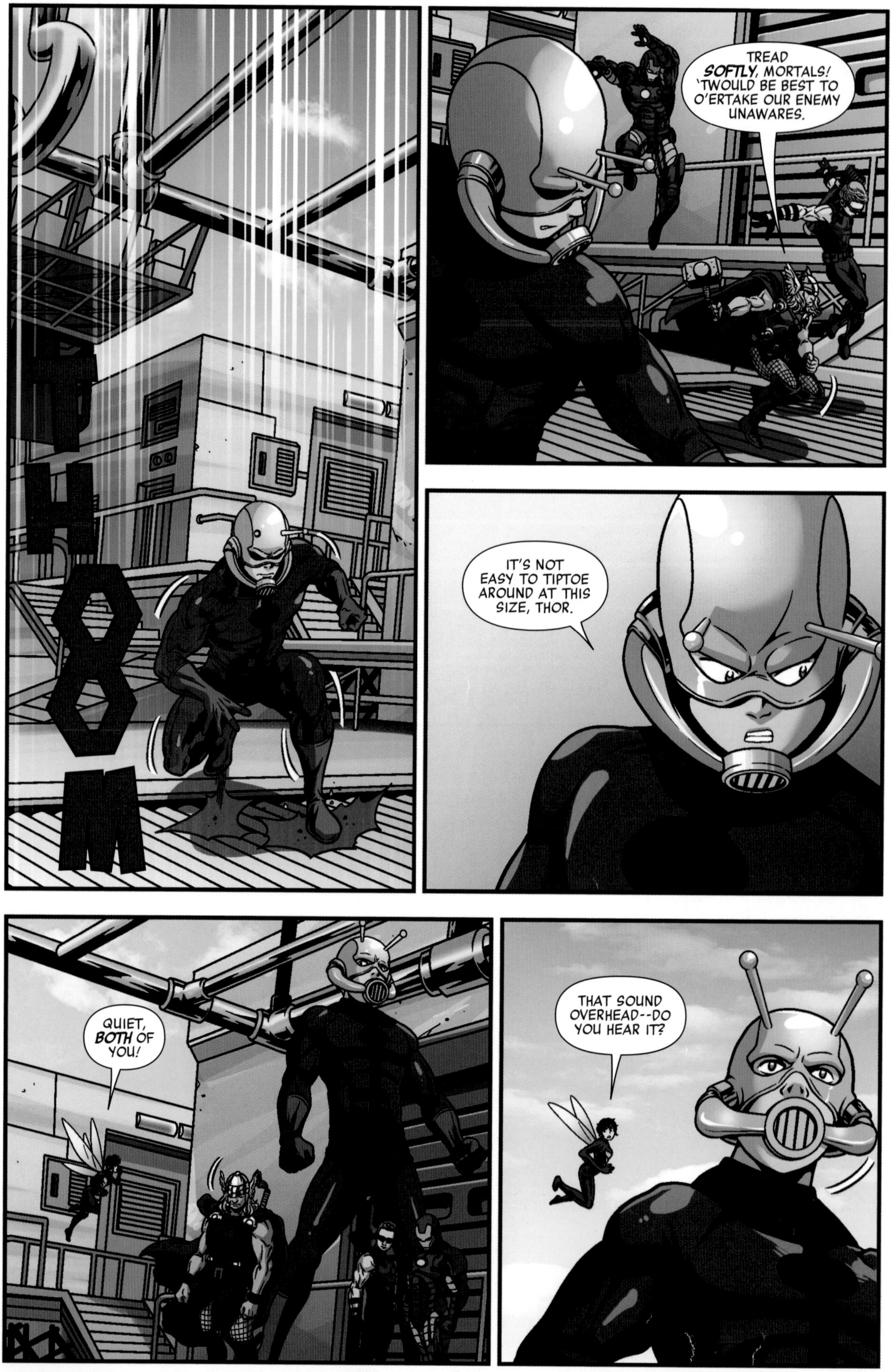
THOOM
TREAD SOFTLY, MORTALS! 'TWOULD BE BEST TO O'ERTAKE OUR ENEMY UNAWARES.
IT'S NOT EASY TO TIPTOE AROUND AT THIS SIZE, THOR.
QUIET, BOTH OF YOU!
THAT SOUND OVERHEAD--DO YOU HEAR IT?

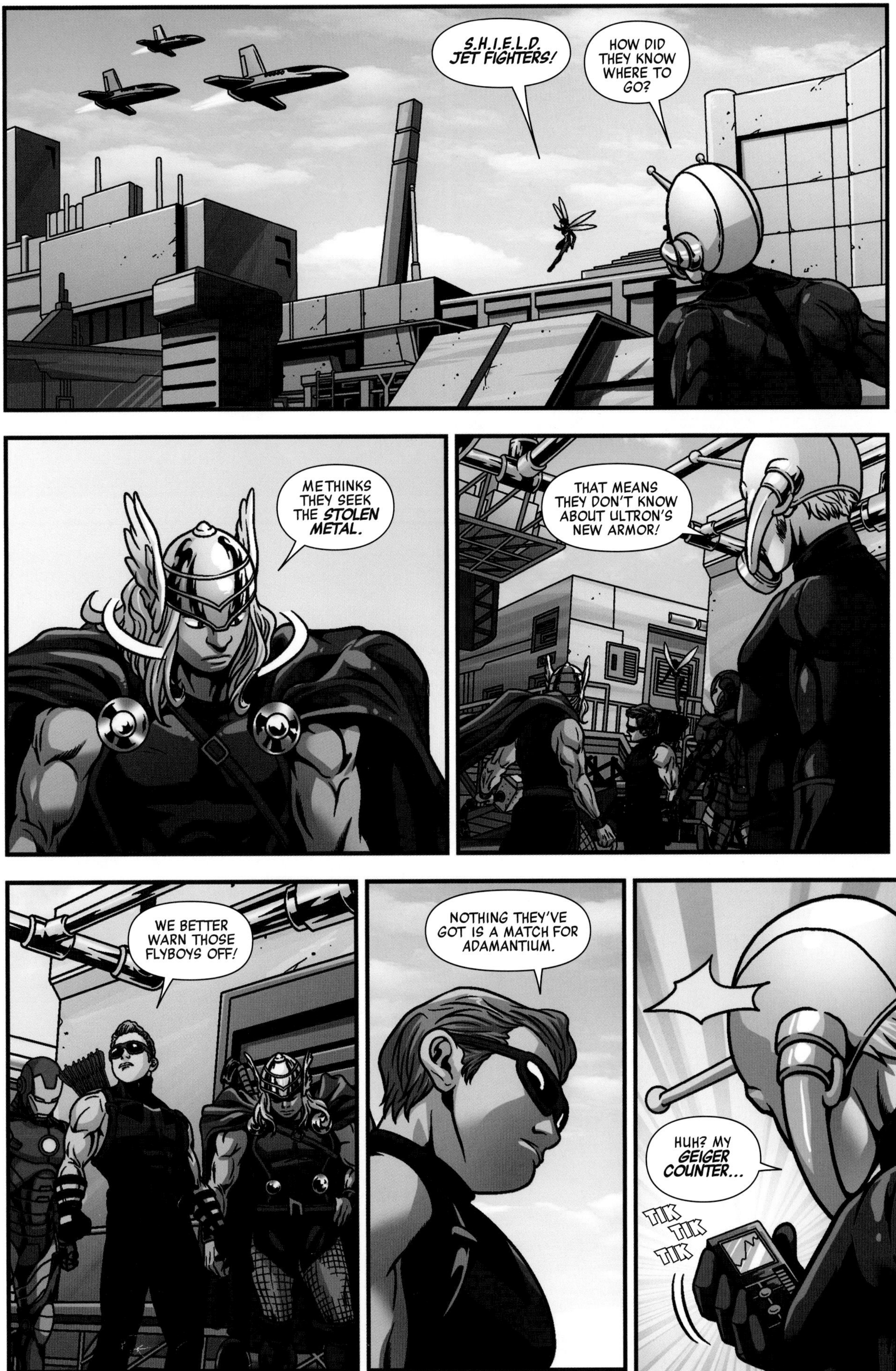
S.H.I.E.L.D. JET FIGHTERS!
HOW DID THEY KNOW WHERE TO GO?
METHINKS THEY SEEK THE STOLEN METAL.
THAT MEANS THEY DON'T KNOW ABOUT ULTRON'S NEW ARMOR!
WE BETTER WARN THOSE FLYBOYS OFF!
NOTHING THEY'VE GOT IS A MATCH FOR ADAMANTIUM.
HUH? MY GEIGER COUNTER...
TIK TIK TIK

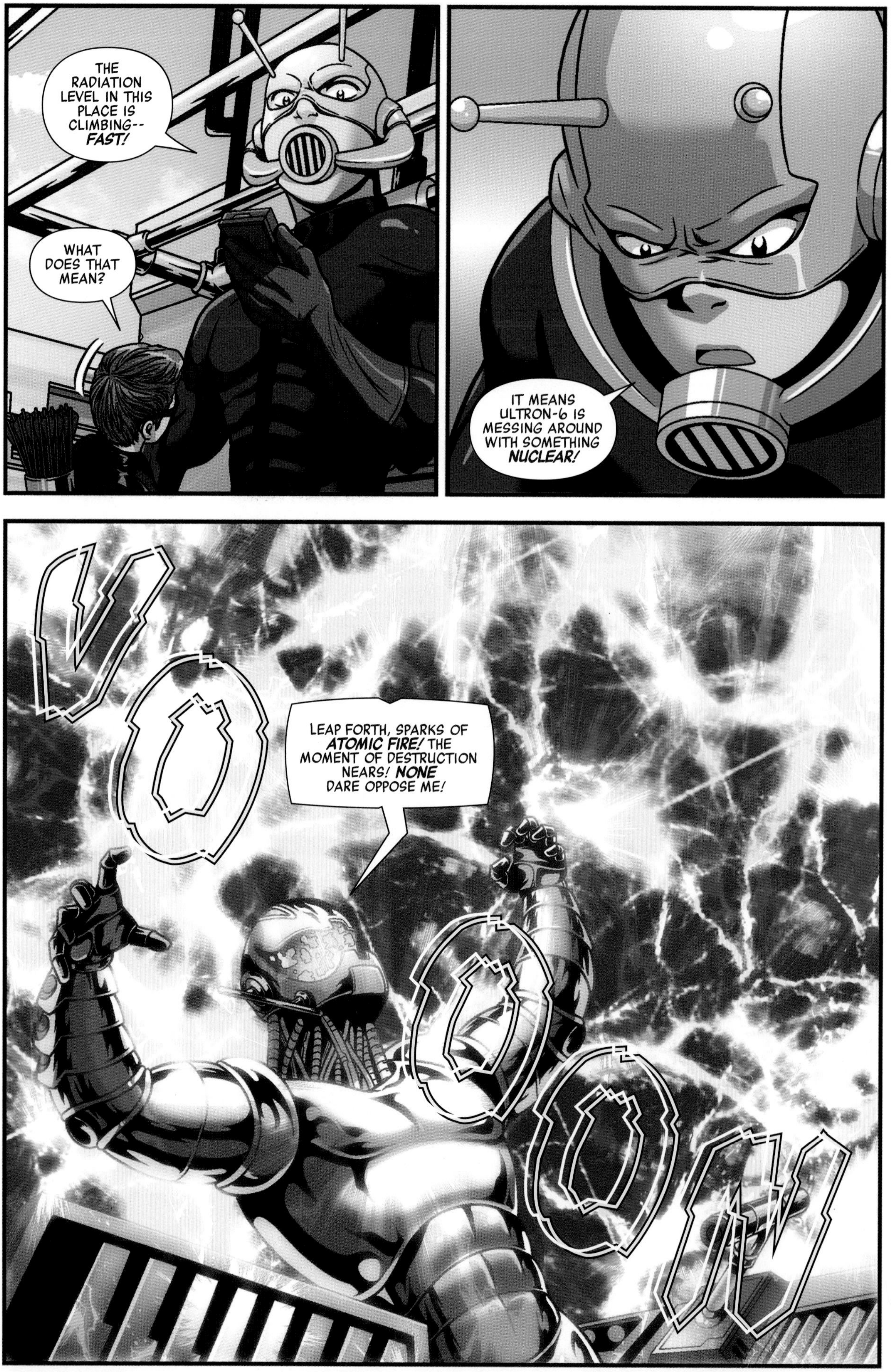
THE RADIATION LEVEL IN THIS PLACE IS CLIMBING-- FAST!
WHAT DOES THAT MEAN?
IT MEANS ULTRON-6 IS MESSING AROUND WITH SOMETHING NUCLEAR!
VOOOOM
LEAP FORTH, SPARKS OF ATOMIC FIRE! THE MOMENT OF DESTRUCTION NEARS! NONE DARE OPPOSE ME!

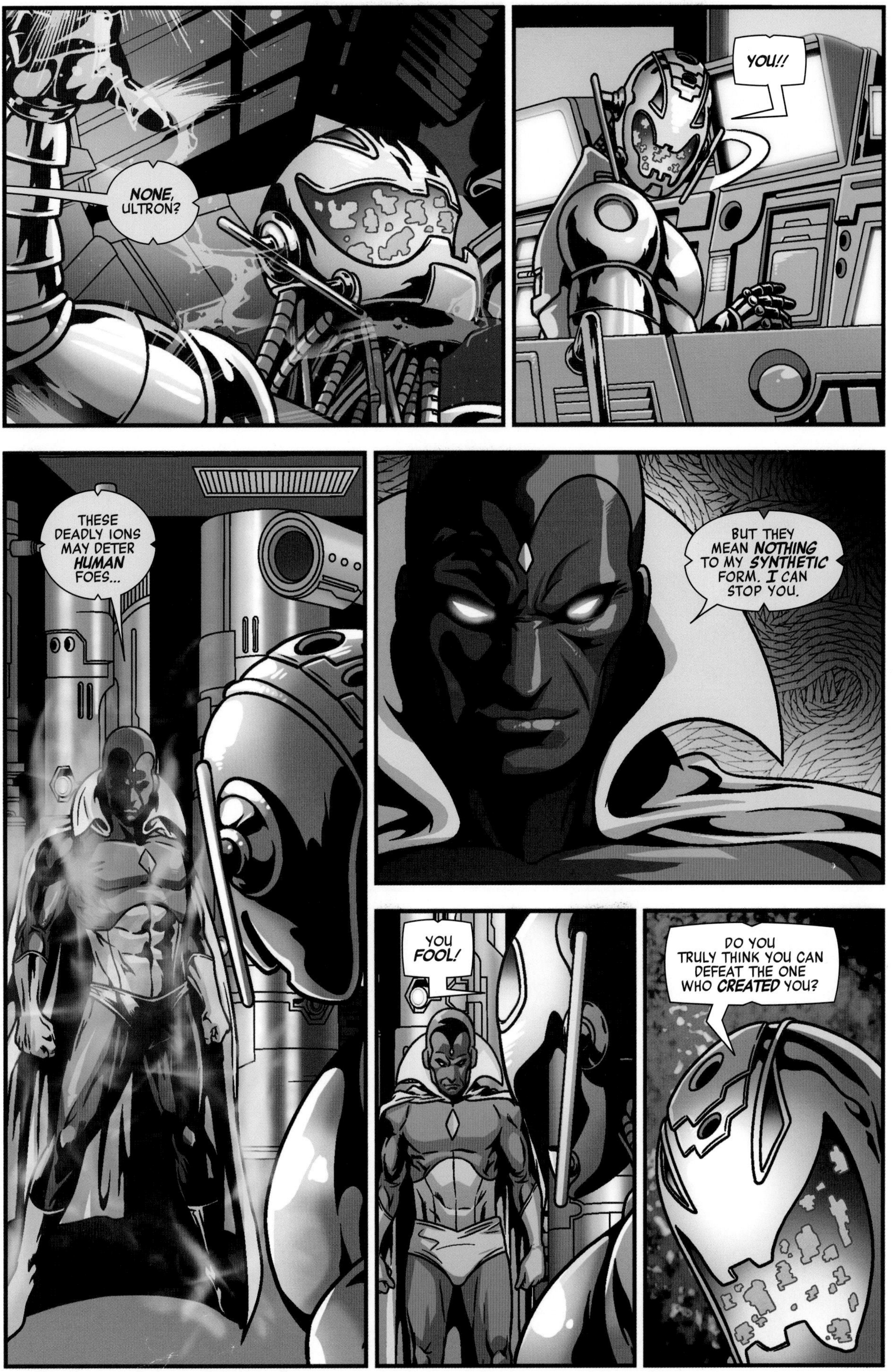
NONE, ULTRON?
YOU!!
THESE DEADLY IONS MAY DETER HUMAN FOES...
BUT THEY MEAN NOTHING TO MY SYNTHETIC FORM. I CAN STOP YOU.
YOU FOOL!
DO YOU TRULY THINK YOU CAN DEFEAT THE ONE WHO CREATED YOU?

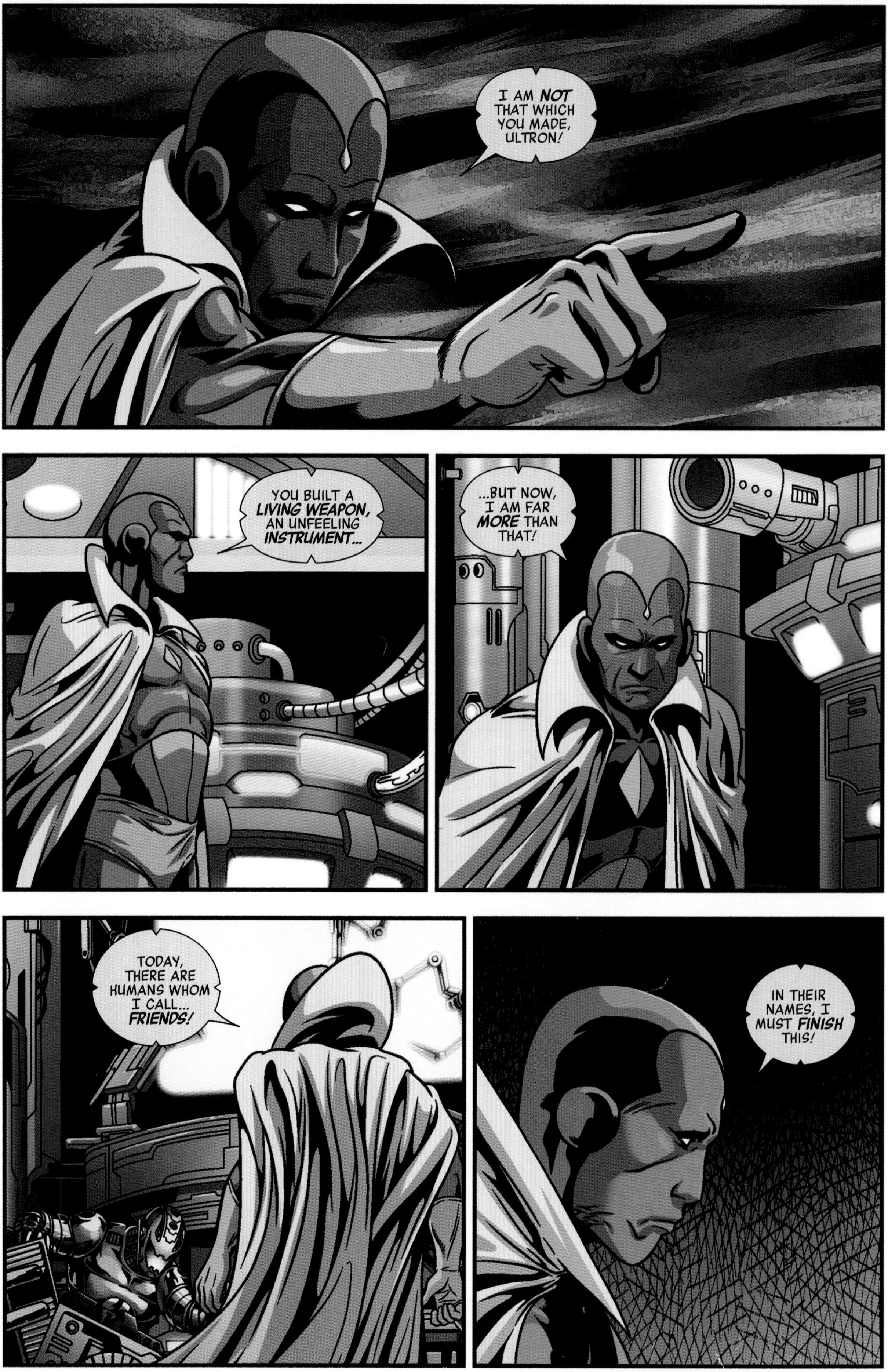
I AM NOT THAT WHICH YOU MADE, ULTRON!
YOU BUILT A LIVING WEAPON, AN UNFEELING INSTRUMENT...
...BUT NOW, I AM FAR MORE THAN THAT!
TODAY, THERE ARE HUMANS WHOM I CALL... FRIENDS!
IN THEIR NAMES, I MUST FINISH THIS!

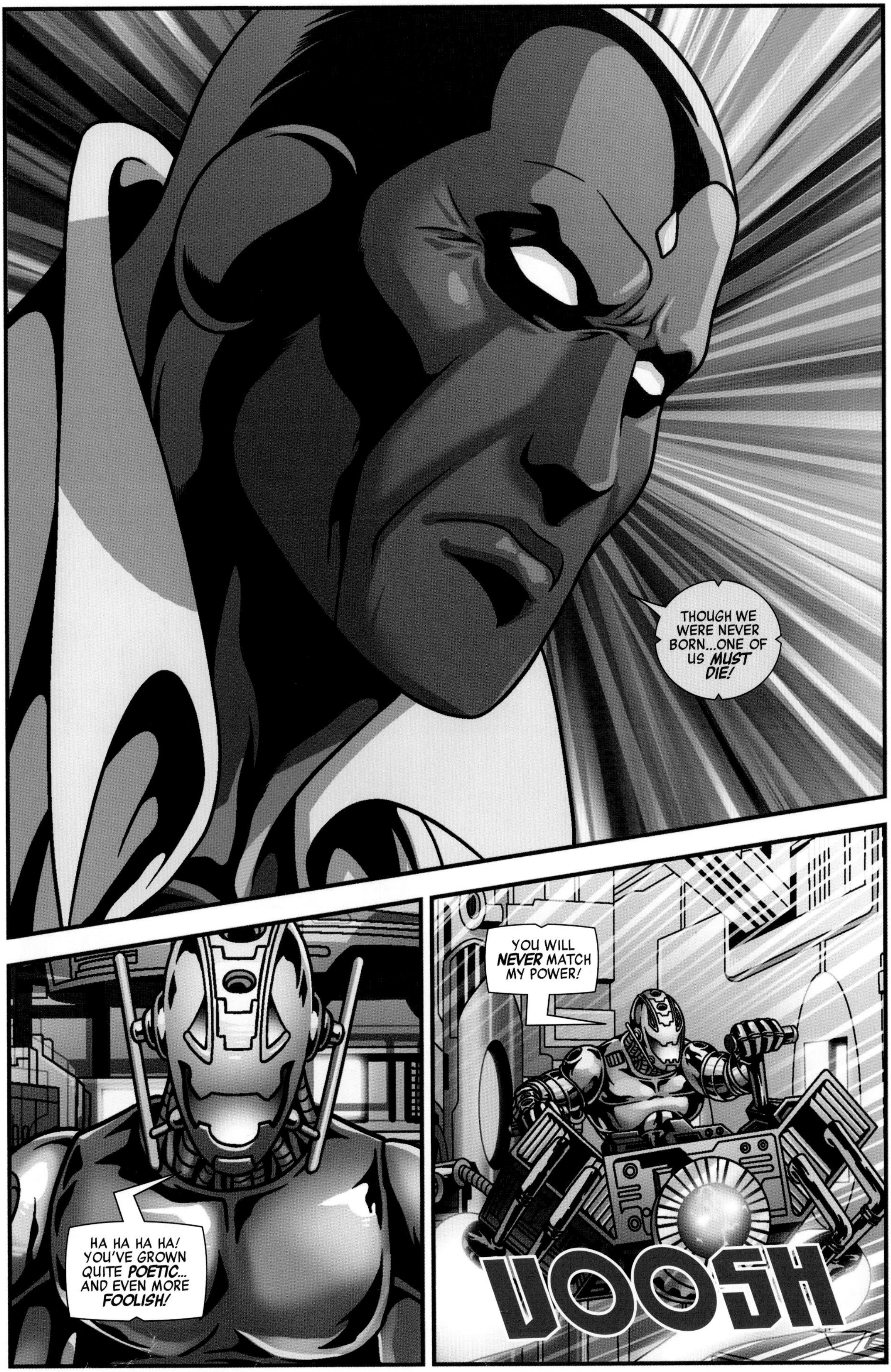
THOUGH WE WERE NEVER BORN...ONE OF US **MUST DIE!**
HA HA HA HA! YOU'VE GROWN QUITE **POETIC**... AND EVEN MORE **FOOLISH!**
YOU WILL **NEVER** MATCH MY POWER!
VOOSH

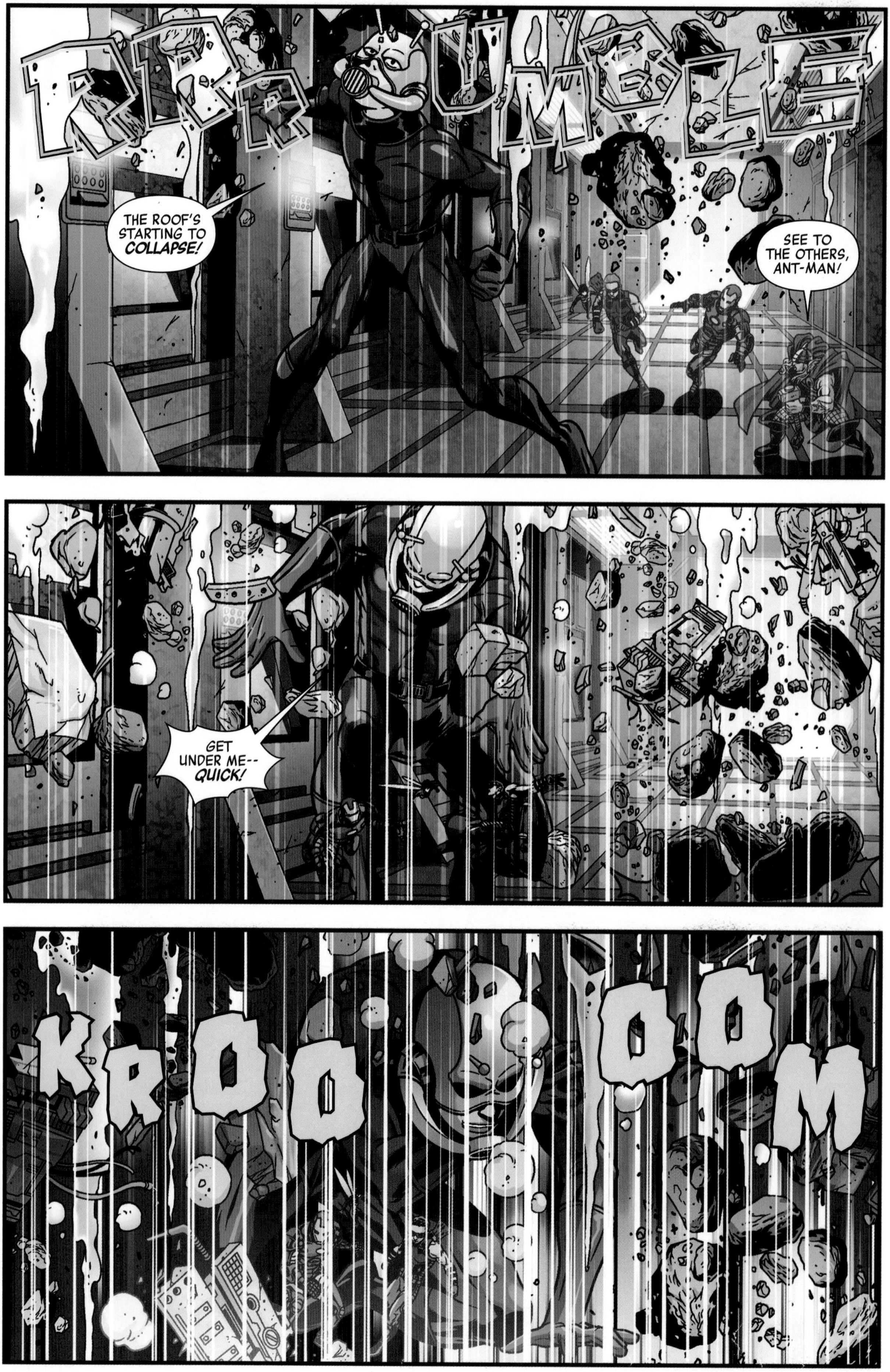
RRRUMBLE
THE ROOF'S STARTING TO *COLLAPSE!*
SEE TO THE OTHERS, ANT-MAN!
GET UNDER ME-- *QUICK!*
KROOOOM

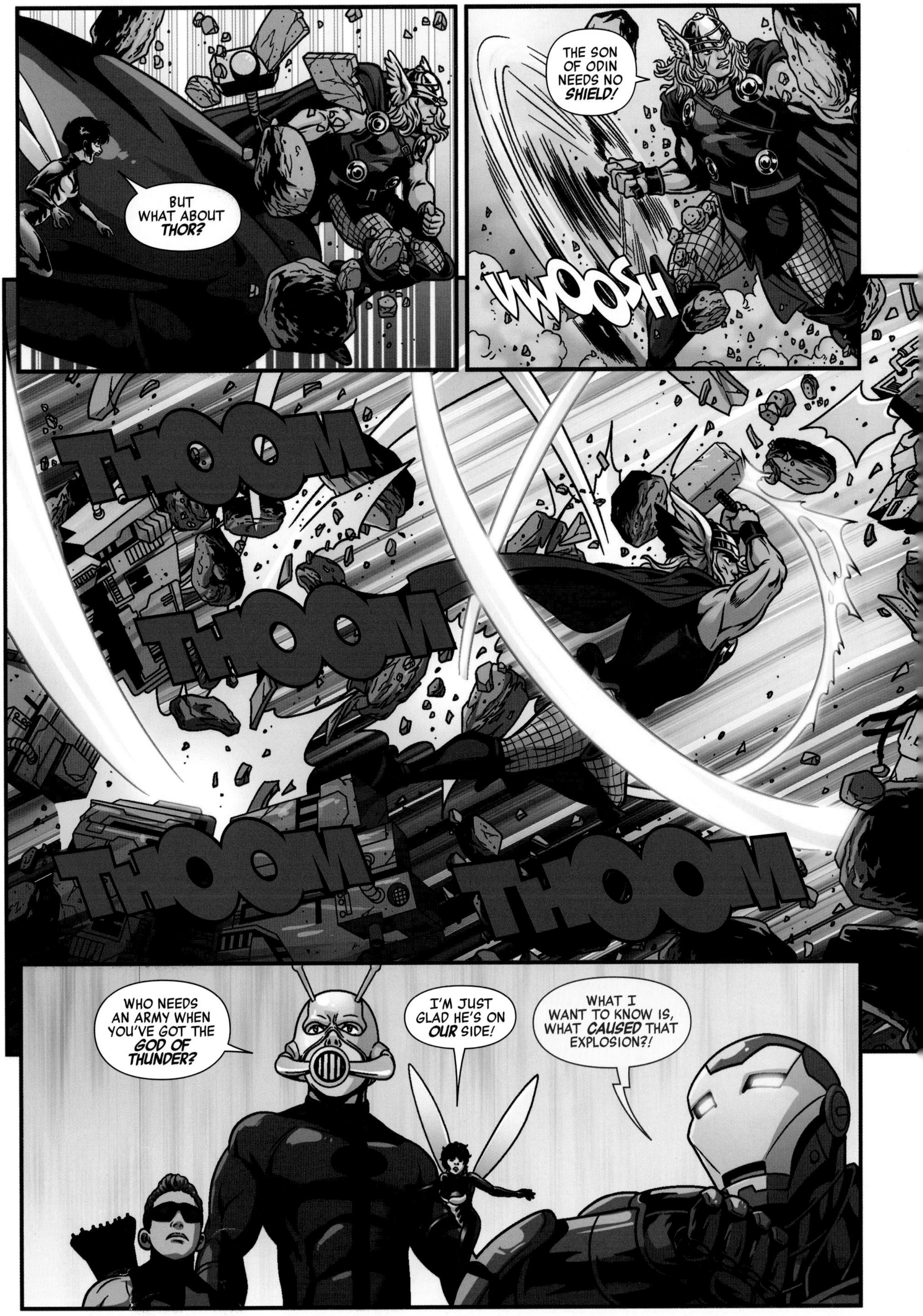
BUT WHAT ABOUT THOR?
THE SON OF ODIN NEEDS NO SHIELD!
VWOOSH
THOOM
THOOM
THOOM
THOOM
WHO NEEDS AN ARMY WHEN YOU'VE GOT THE GOD OF THUNDER?
I'M JUST GLAD HE'S ON OUR SIDE!
WHAT I WANT TO KNOW IS, WHAT CAUSED THAT EXPLOSION?!

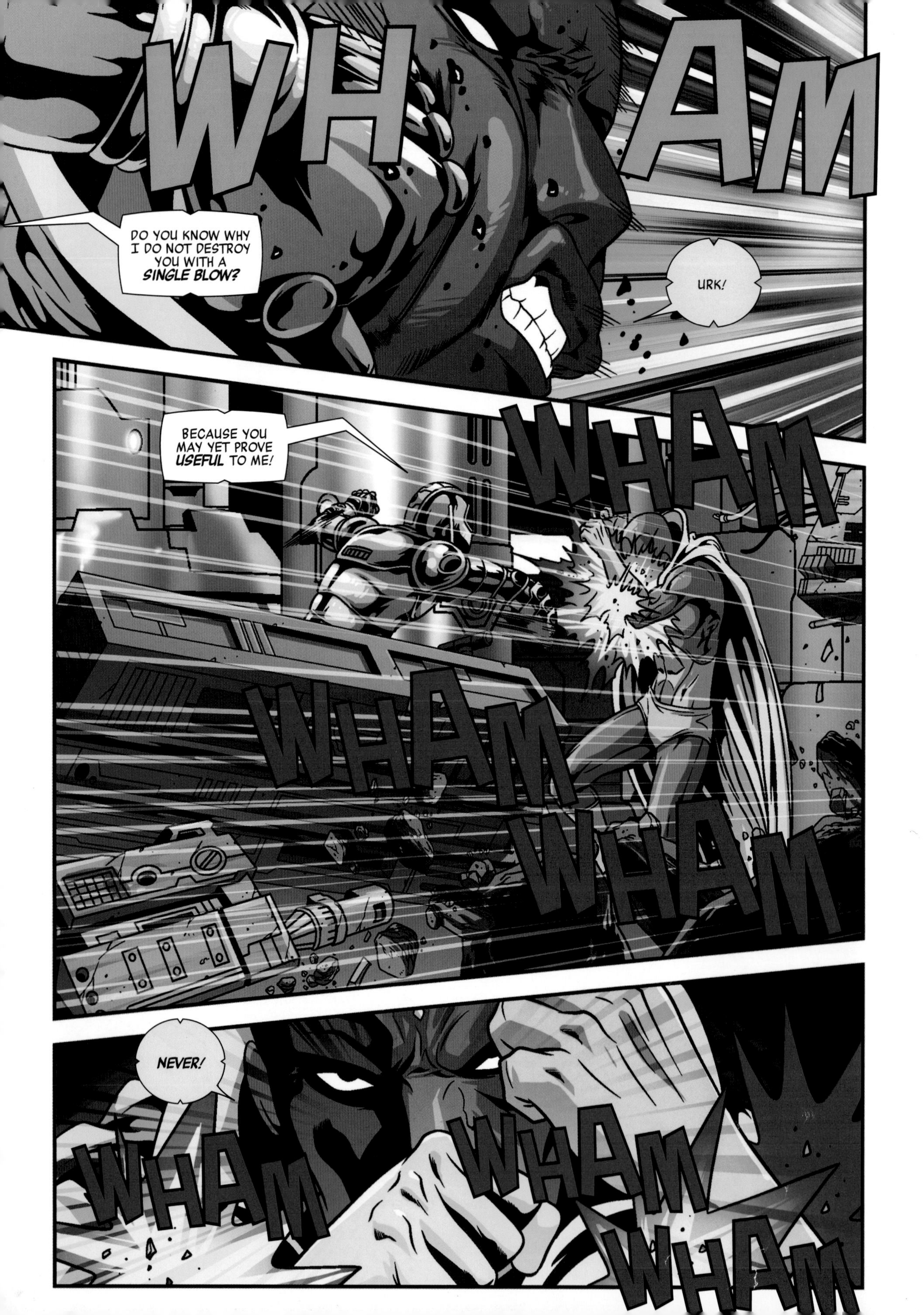
WH AM
DO YOU KNOW WHY I DO NOT DESTROY YOU WITH A SINGLE BLOW?
URK!
BECAUSE YOU MAY YET PROVE USEFUL TO ME!
WHAM
WHAM
WHAM
NEVER!
WHAM
WHAM
WHAM

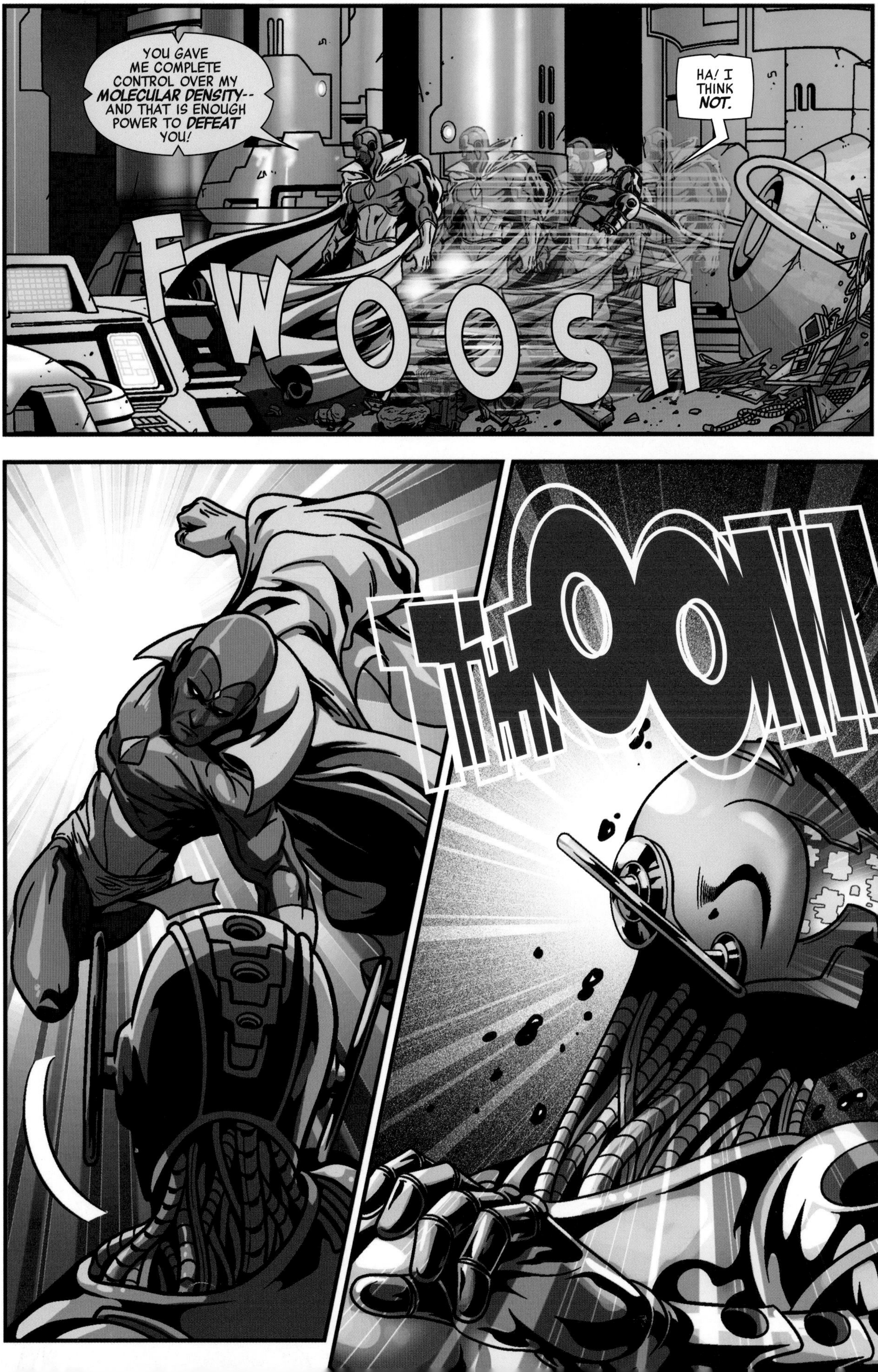
YOU GAVE ME COMPLETE CONTROL OVER MY MOLECULAR DENSITY-- AND THAT IS ENOUGH POWER TO DEFEAT YOU!
HA! I THINK NOT.
FWOOSH
THOOMM

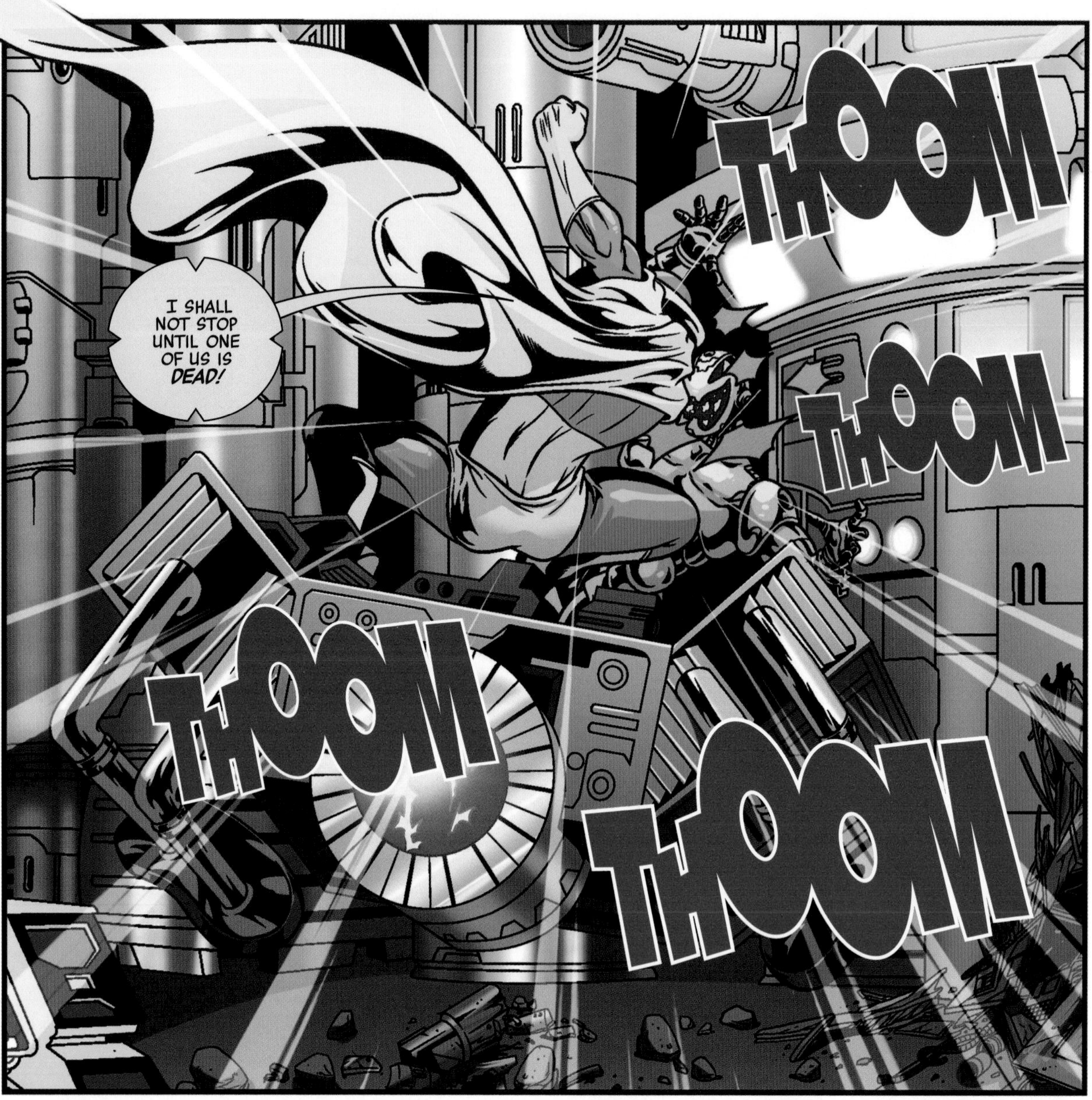
I SHALL NOT STOP UNTIL ONE OF US IS *DEAD!*
THOOM
THOOM
THOOM
THOOM

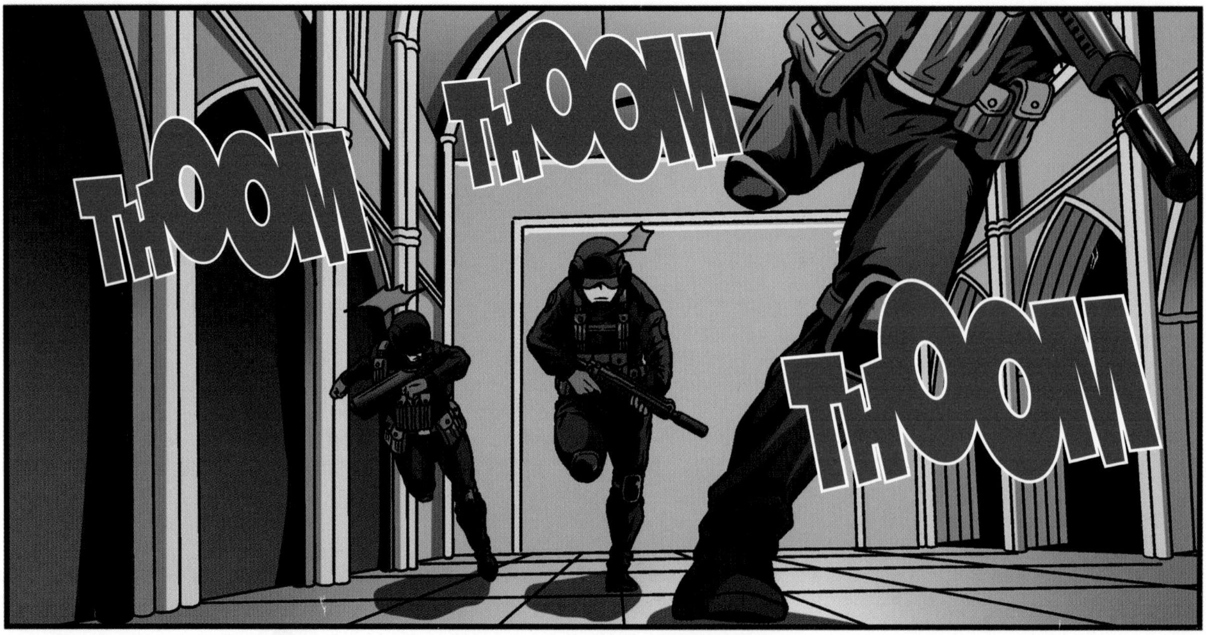
THOOM
THOOM
THOOM

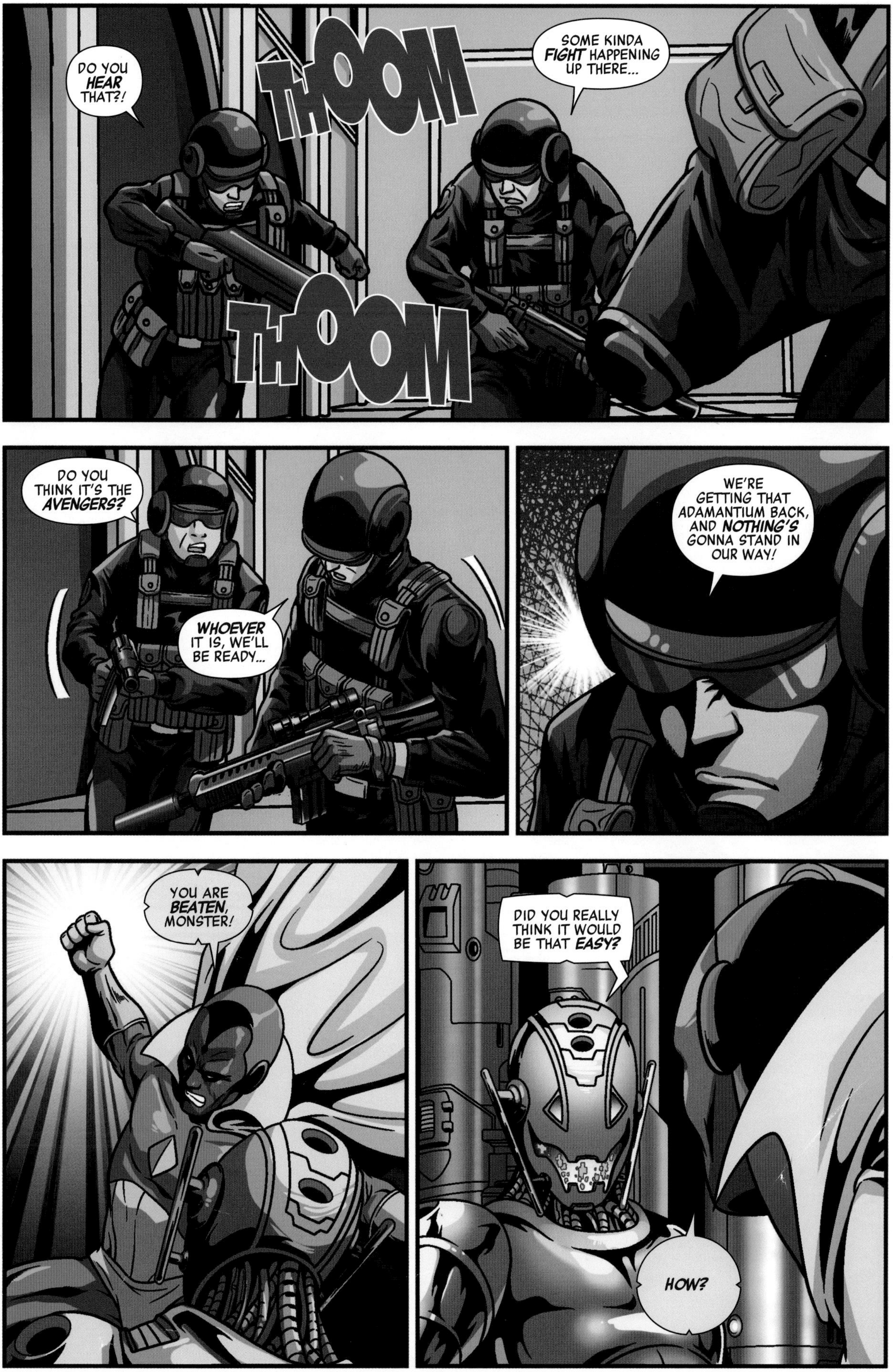
DO YOU HEAR THAT?!
THOOM
SOME KINDA FIGHT HAPPENING UP THERE...
THOOM
DO YOU THINK IT'S THE AVENGERS?
WHOEVER IT IS, WE'LL BE READY...
WE'RE GETTING THAT ADAMANTIUM BACK, AND NOTHING'S GONNA STAND IN OUR WAY!
YOU ARE BEATEN, MONSTER!
DID YOU REALLY THINK IT WOULD BE THAT EASY?
HOW?

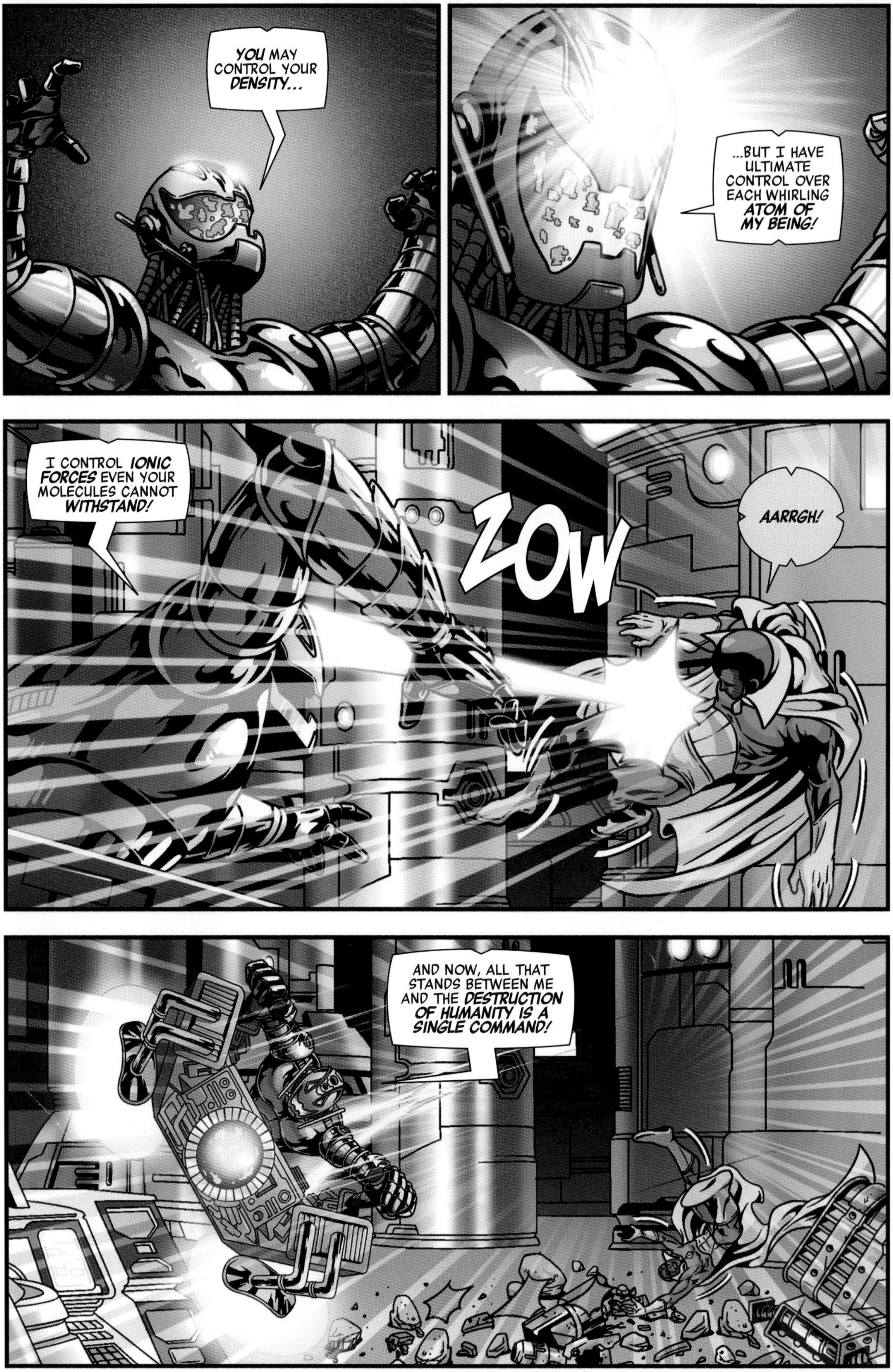
YOU MAY CONTROL YOUR DENSITY...
...BUT I HAVE ULTIMATE CONTROL OVER EACH WHIRLING ATOM OF MY BEING!
I CONTROL IONIC FORCES EVEN YOUR MOLECULES CANNOT WITHSTAND!
ZOW
AARRGH!
AND NOW, ALL THAT STANDS BETWEEN ME AND THE DESTRUCTION OF HUMANITY IS A SINGLE COMMAND!

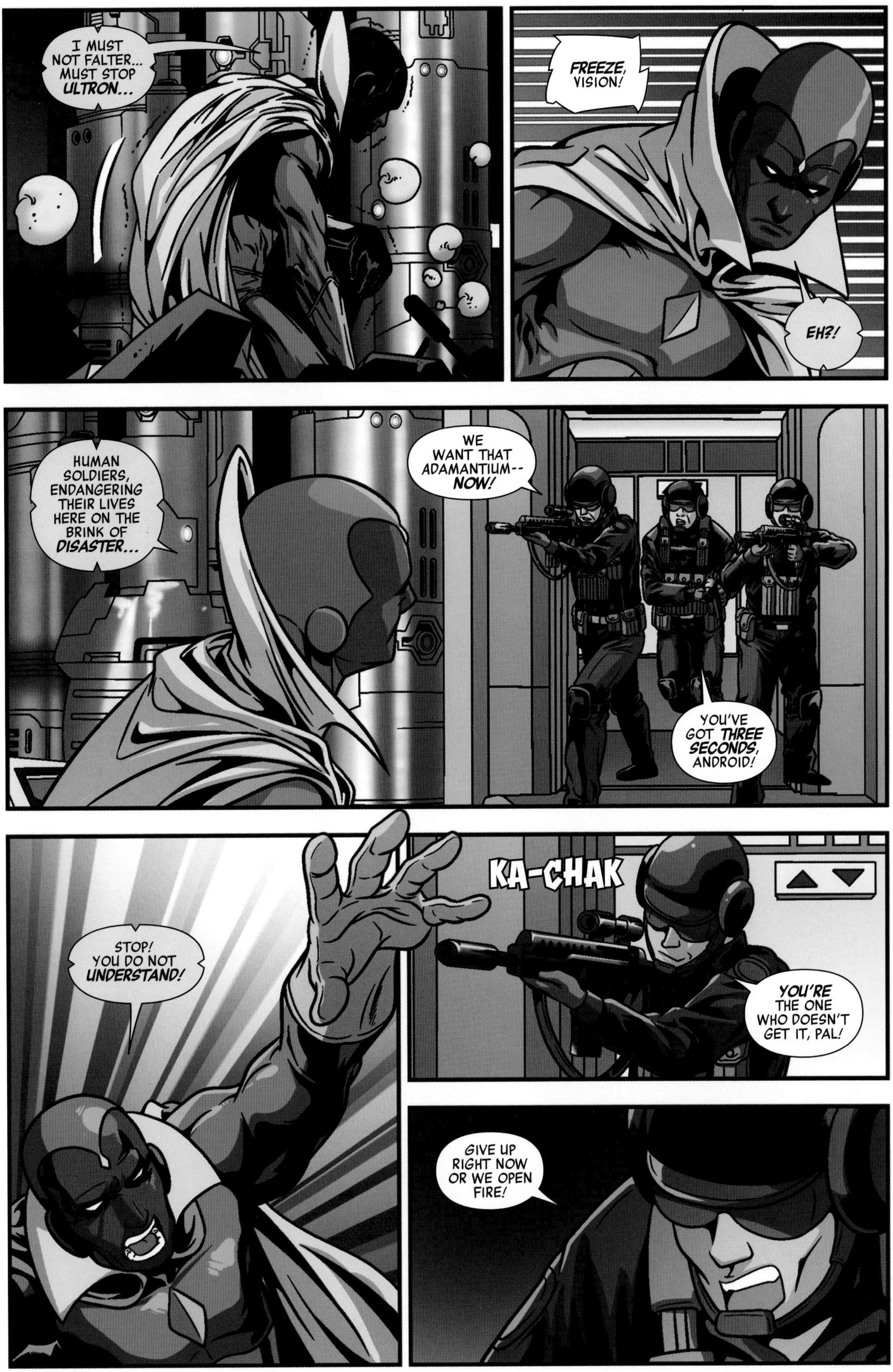
I MUST NOT FALTER... MUST STOP ULTRON...
FREEZE, VISION!
EH?!
HUMAN SOLDIERS, ENDANGERING THEIR LIVES HERE ON THE BRINK OF DISASTER...
WE WANT THAT ADAMANTIUM-- NOW!
YOU'VE GOT THREE SECONDS, ANDROID!
STOP! YOU DO NOT UNDERSTAND!
KA-CHAK
YOU'RE THE ONE WHO DOESN'T GET IT, PAL!
GIVE UP RIGHT NOW OR WE OPEN FIRE!

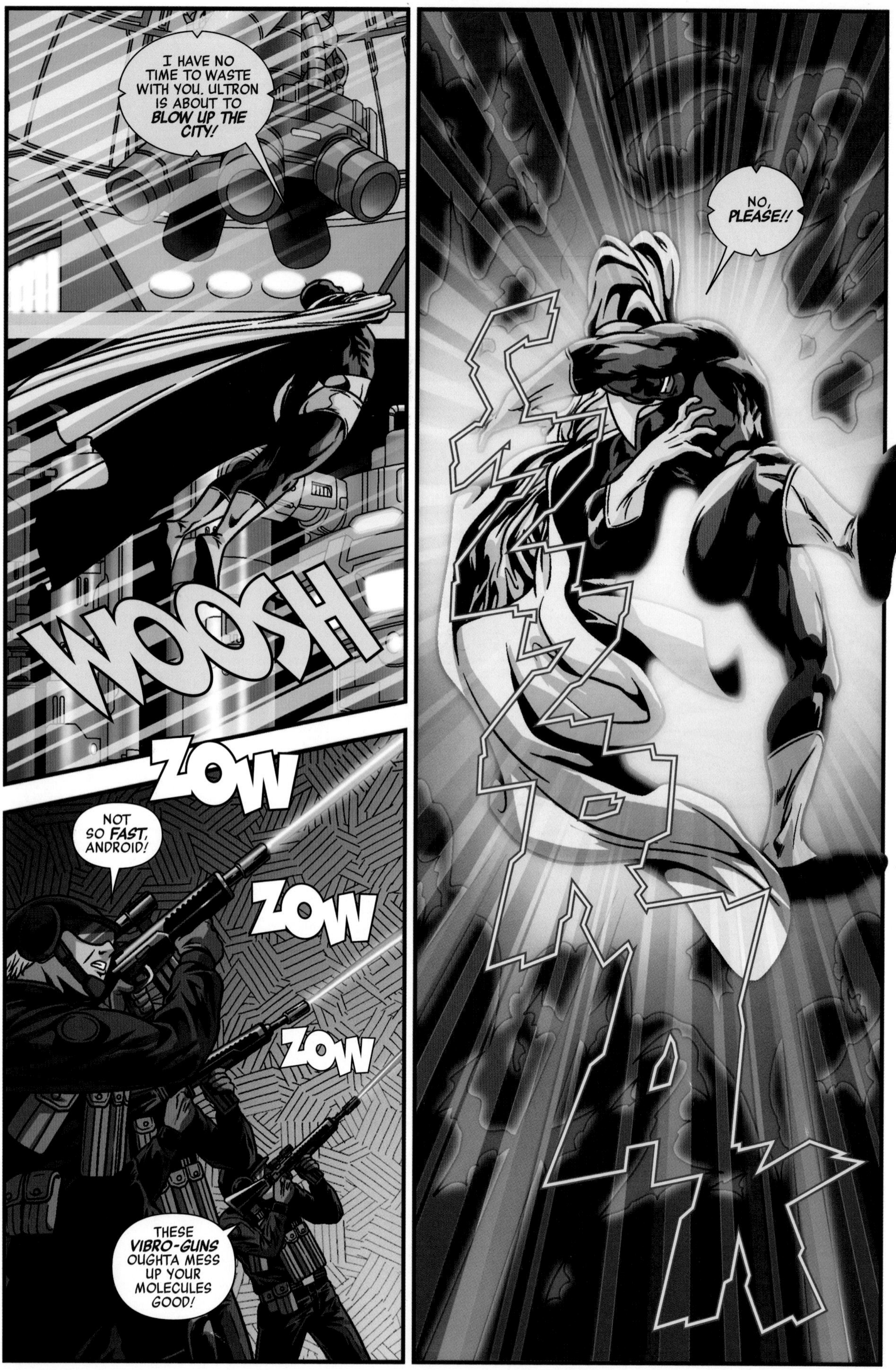
I HAVE NO TIME TO WASTE WITH YOU. ULTRON IS ABOUT TO BLOW UP THE CITY!
WOOSH
ZOW
NOT SO FAST, ANDROID!
ZOW
ZOW
THESE VIBRO-GUNS OUGHTA MESS UP YOUR MOLECULES GOOD!
NO, PLEASE!!

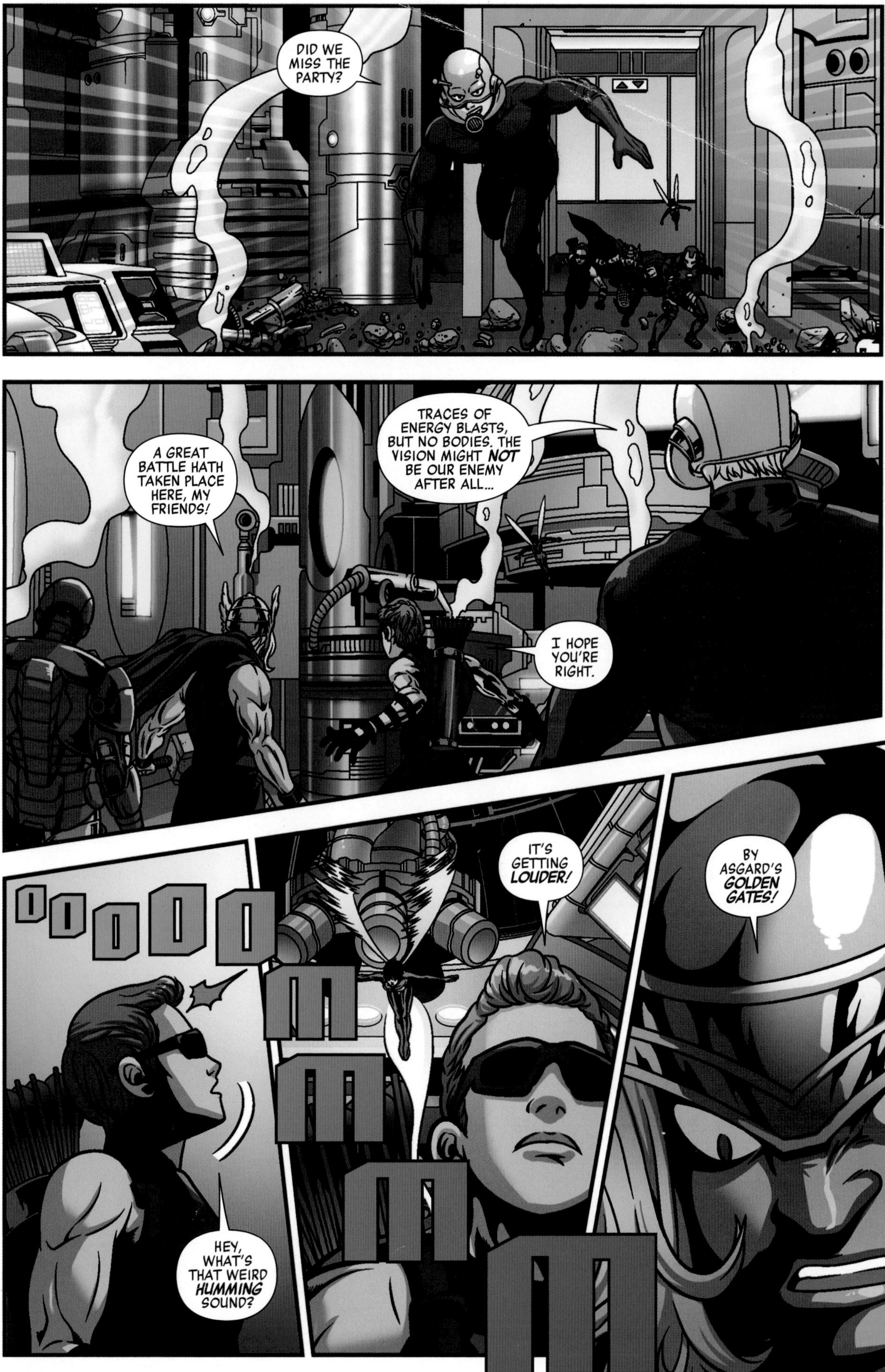
DID WE MISS THE PARTY?
A GREAT BATTLE HATH TAKEN PLACE HERE, MY FRIENDS!
TRACES OF ENERGY BLASTS, BUT NO BODIES. THE VISION MIGHT NOT BE OUR ENEMY AFTER ALL...
I HOPE YOU'RE RIGHT.
OOOOOMMMM
HEY, WHAT'S THAT WEIRD HUMMING SOUND?
IT'S GETTING LOUDER!
BY ASGARD'S GOLDEN GATES!

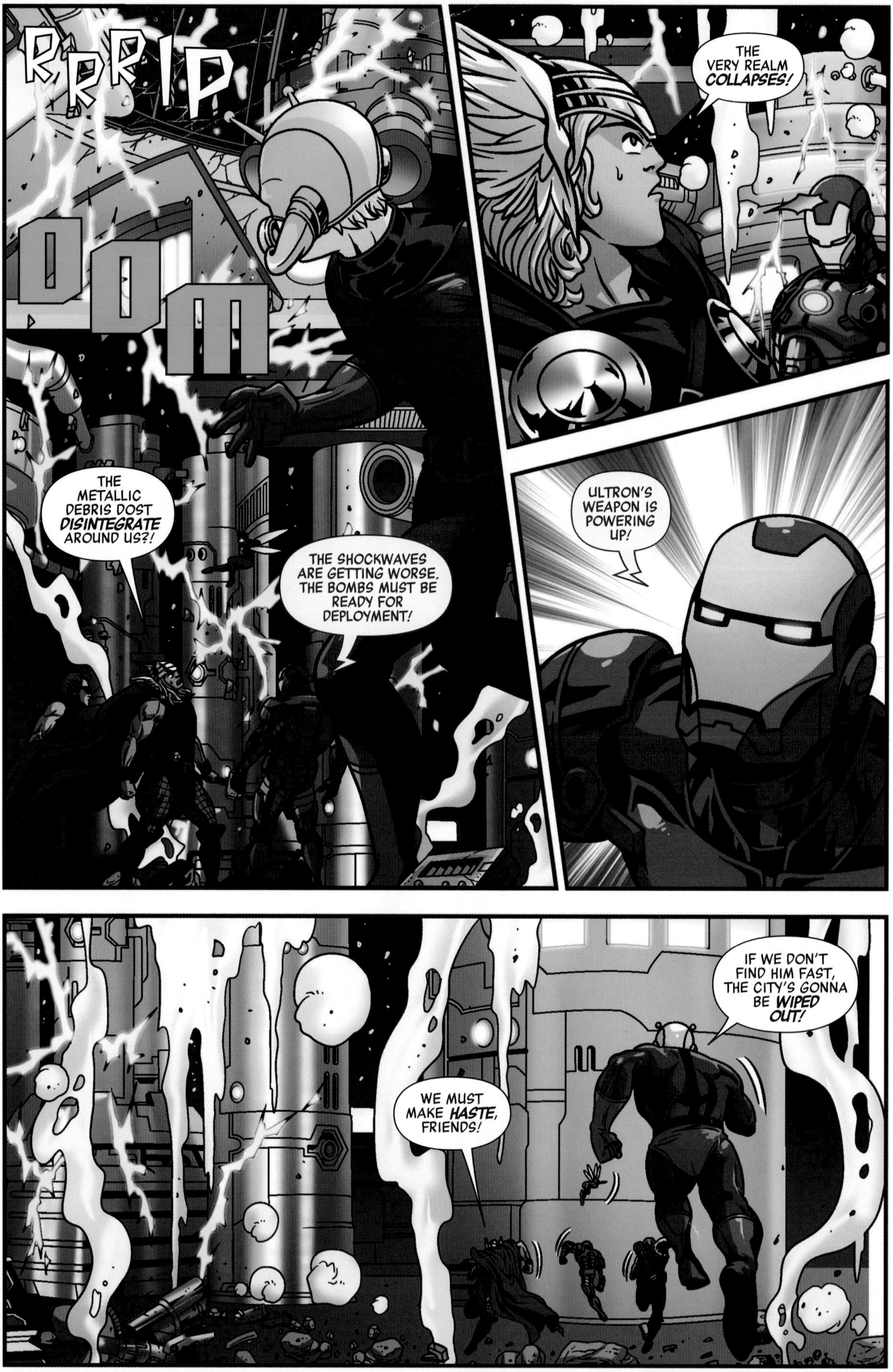
RRRIP
DOOM
THE VERY REALM COLLAPSES!
ULTRON'S WEAPON IS POWERING UP!
THE METALLIC DEBRIS DOST DISINTEGRATE AROUND US?!
THE SHOCKWAVES ARE GETTING WORSE. THE BOMBS MUST BE READY FOR DEPLOYMENT!
IF WE DON'T FIND HIM FAST, THE CITY'S GONNA BE WIPED OUT!
WE MUST MAKE HASTE, FRIENDS!

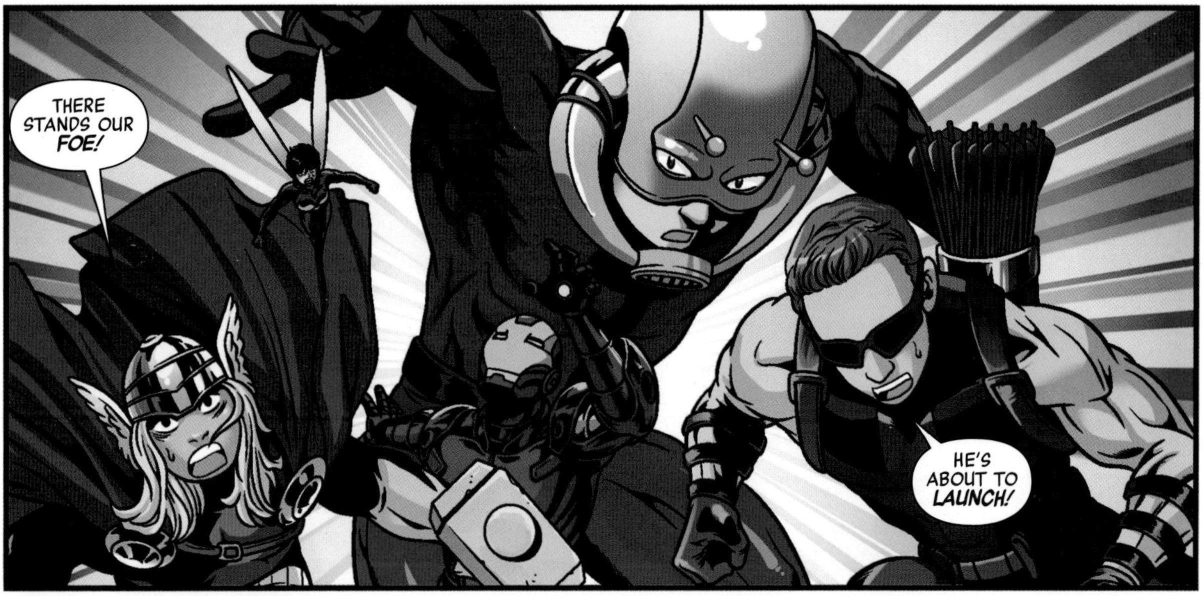
THERE STANDS OUR FOE!
HE'S ABOUT TO LAUNCH!

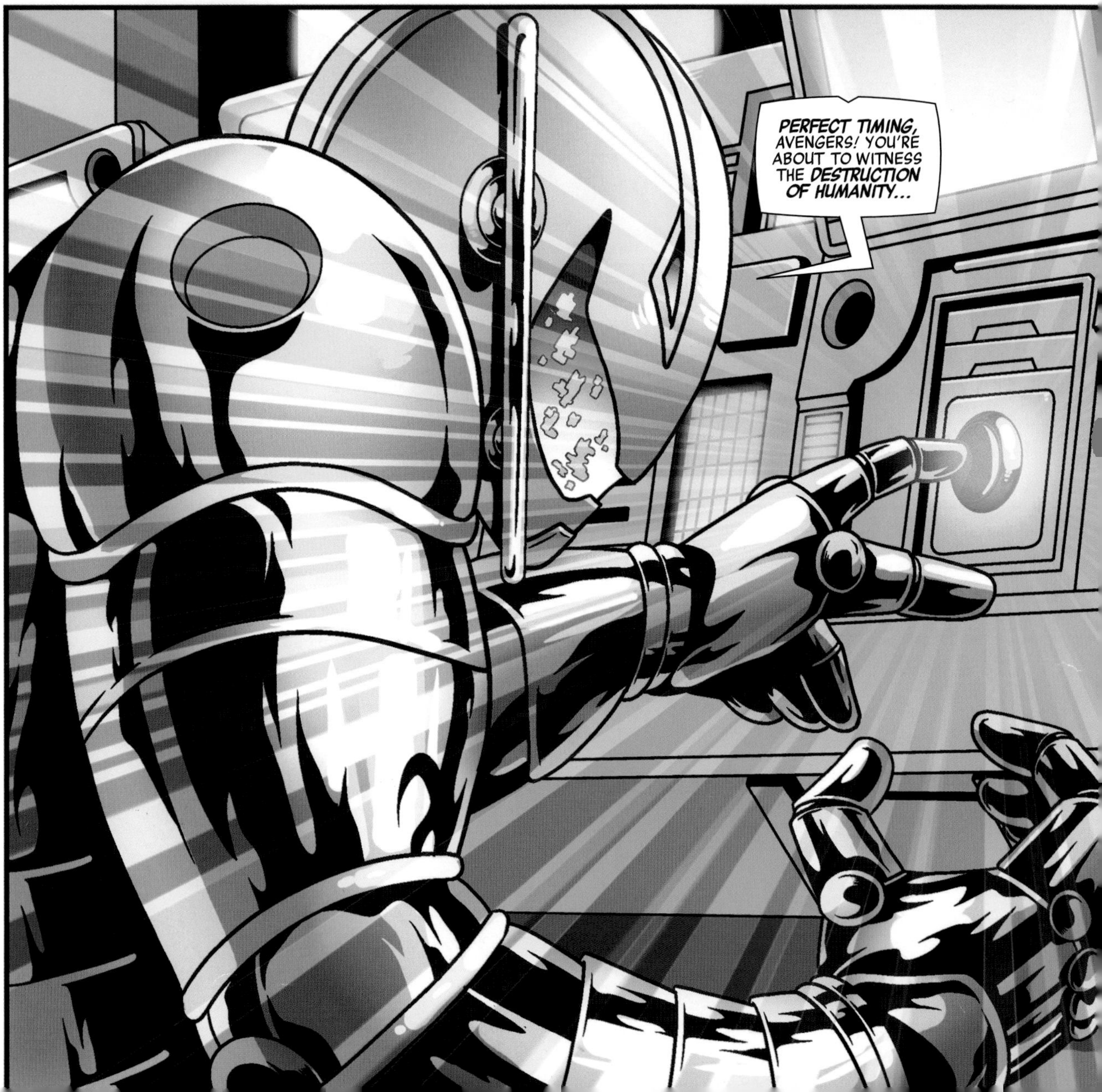
PERFECT TIMING, AVENGERS! YOU'RE ABOUT TO WITNESS THE DESTRUCTION OF HUMANITY...

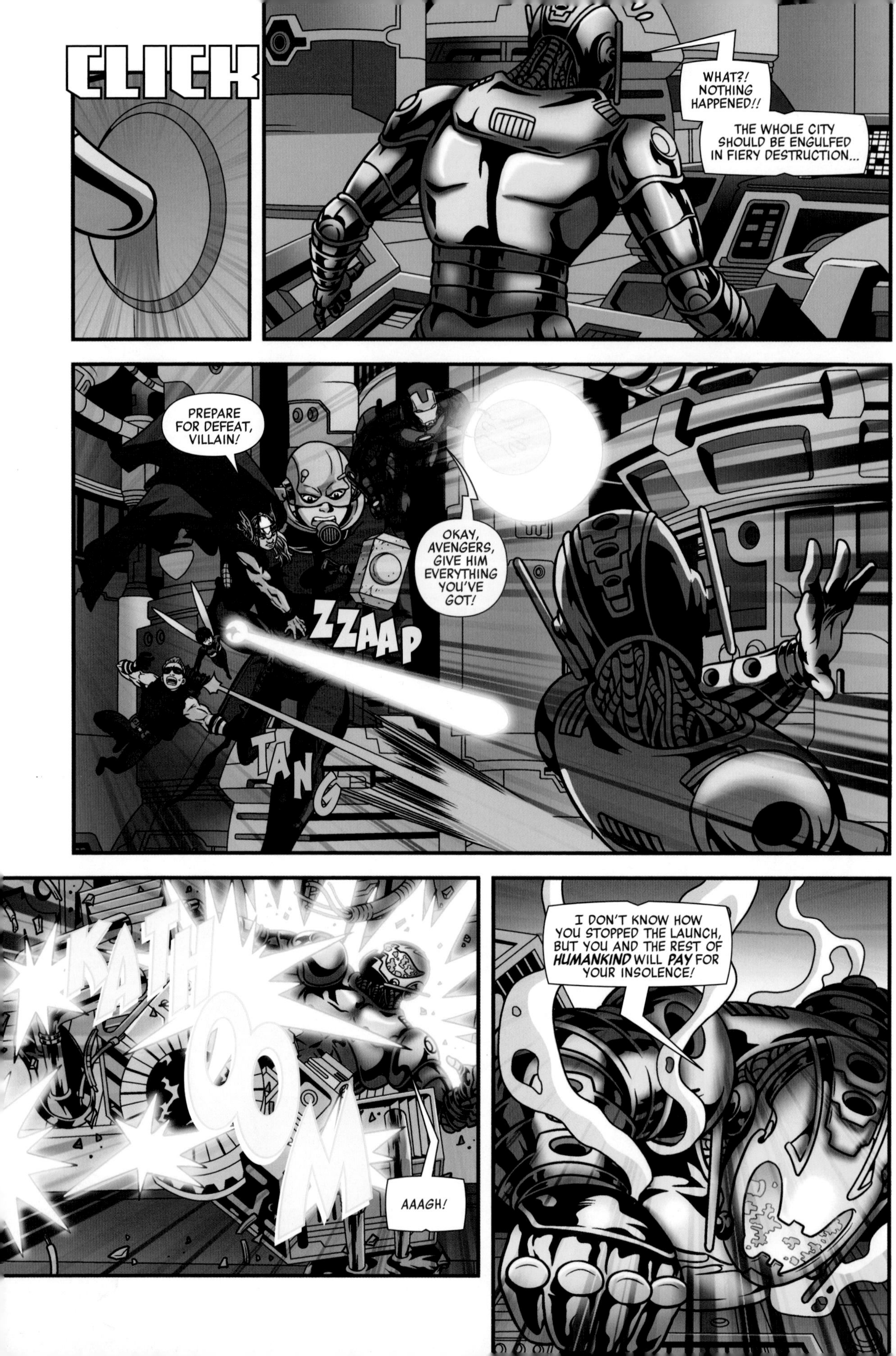
CLICK
WHAT?! NOTHING HAPPENED!!
THE WHOLE CITY SHOULD BE ENGULFED IN FIERY DESTRUCTION...
PREPARE FOR DEFEAT, VILLAIN!
OKAY, AVENGERS, GIVE HIM EVERYTHING YOU'VE GOT!
ZZZAAP
TANG
KATHOOM
AAAGH!
I DON'T KNOW HOW YOU STOPPED THE LAUNCH, BUT YOU AND THE REST OF HUMANKIND WILL PAY FOR YOUR INSOLENCE!

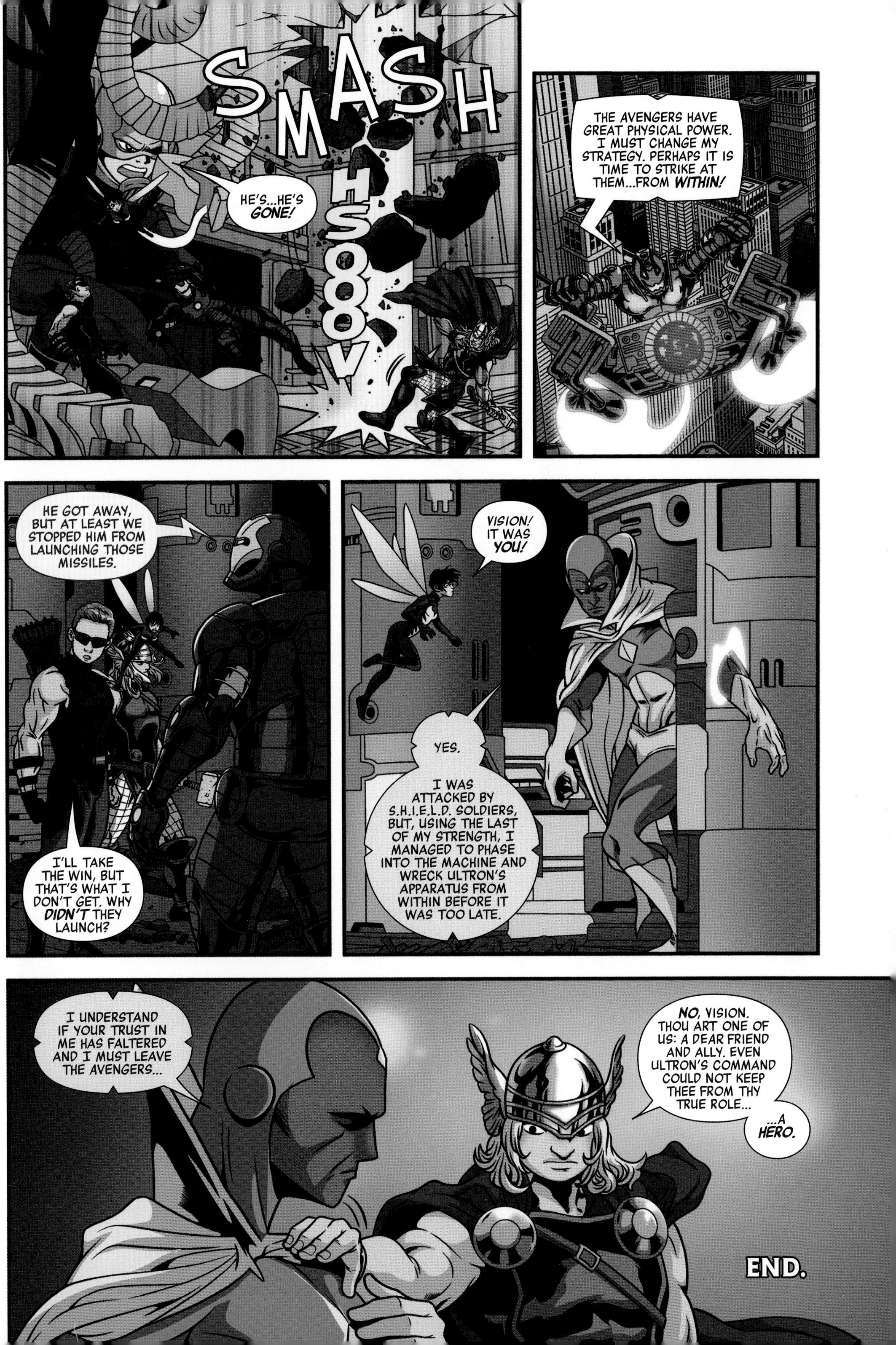
SMASH
HE'S...HE'S GONE!
VOOSH
THE AVENGERS HAVE GREAT PHYSICAL POWER. I MUST CHANGE MY STRATEGY. PERHAPS IT IS TIME TO STRIKE AT THEM...FROM WITHIN!
HE GOT AWAY, BUT AT LEAST WE STOPPED HIM FROM LAUNCHING THOSE MISSILES.
I'LL TAKE THE WIN, BUT THAT'S WHAT I DON'T GET. WHY DIDN'T THEY LAUNCH?
VISION! IT WAS YOU!
YES.
I WAS ATTACKED BY S.H.I.E.L.D. SOLDIERS, BUT, USING THE LAST OF MY STRENGTH, I MANAGED TO PHASE INTO THE MACHINE AND WRECK ULTRON'S APPARATUS FROM WITHIN BEFORE IT WAS TOO LATE.
I UNDERSTAND IF YOUR TRUST IN ME HAS FALTERED AND I MUST LEAVE THE AVENGERS...
NO, VISION. THOU ART ONE OF US: A DEAR FRIEND AND ALLY. EVEN ULTRON'S COMMAND COULD NOT KEEP THEE FROM THY TRUE ROLE...
...A HERO.
END.

AVENGERS K
AVENGERS VS. ULTRON

COLLECT THEM ALL!
Set of 6 Hardcover Books ISBN: 978-1-61479-567-4

AVENGERS K #1
AVENGERS VS. ULTRON
MARVEL

Hardcover Book ISBN
978-1-61479-568-1

AVENGERS K #2
AVENGERS VS. ULTRON
MARVEL

Hardcover Book ISBN
978-1-61479-569-8

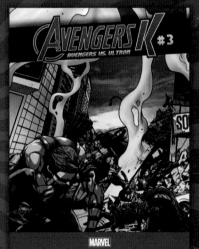

AVENGERS K #3
AVENGERS VS. ULTRON
MARVEL

Hardcover Book ISBN
978-1-61479-570-4

AVENGERS K #4
AVENGERS VS. ULTRON
MARVEL

Hardcover Book ISBN

AVENGERS K #5
AVENGERS VS. ULTRON
MARVEL

Hardcover Book ISBN

AVENGERS K #6
AVENGERS VS. ULTRON
MARVEL

Hardcover Book ISBN